CW00722993

INTO THE ETHER

Andrew Whitehead

Raider Publishing International

New York   London   Cape Town

© 2011 Andrew Whitehead

All rights reserved. No part of this book may be reproduced stored in a retrieval system or transmitted in any form by any means without the prior written permission of the publisher, except by a reviewer who may quote brief passages in a review to be printed in a newspaper, magazine or journal.

First Printing

The views, content and descriptions in this book do not represent the views of Raider Publishing International. Some of the content may be offensive to some readers and they are to be advised. Objections to the content in this book should be directed towards the author and owner of the intellectual property rights as registered with their local government.

All characters portrayed in this book are fictitious and any resemblance to persons living or dead is purely coincidental.

ISBN: 978-1-61667-381-9

Published By Raider Publishing International
www.RaiderPublishing.com
New York London Cape Town
Printed in the United States of America and the United Kingdom

Thanks to all those who have given encouragement and constructive criticism but, most of all, to Megan.

INTO THE ETHER

Andrew Whitehead

1

Birthday Party

It is Thursday the 16th and I am sitting in the exam hall near the end of the allotted time. I read through my exam paper and made a few minor corrections, which should save me a couple of marks, and I've even checked that I'd spelt my own name correctly: Edmund Decovny stared back at me. Good! At least I managed to get that bit right. So, I walked out of the exam hall at 4 pm on Thursday knowing I would have no more school work for nearly three months, having just finished my final AS exam. This one was in English and I felt pretty confident, as it is my best subject and the right questions came up. *Thank you, God!*

Friday is my 17th birthday, but, more importantly, it is the day I take my driving test. In anticipation of my passing – at least, one day – my parents had bought me an old car for my birthday. When I say old, I mean it's so old they don't even make them any more, but I just love the image of a real mini. Yes, they are leaky and very unreliable, but it looks so cool riding around in one. It is just plain blue, but, once I've finished doing it up, it will have a Union Jack on its roof and wing mirrors. I must get a 'BMW free' sticker too! The date for my test has been booked long ago and I have had the advantage that my uncle has a small business on a private industrial estate where I have been able to practice driving before I turned the legal age to drive on the public highway. I approached the test centre with a mixture of confidence and trepidation. My instructor says he is pretty confident, but he probably says that to all his students who are about to take their tests. Even so, I was very nervous and thought about how my birthday present would go to waste if I failed.

My father had taken me around the test course a few times, so I knew the layout and what was expected of me. The first pull away went fine and I'm sure I checked the mirror and looked behind me. Soon I was told to stop on a hill and then pull away again. No problem! Then I was reversing around a corner. I managed to do it without going into the other lane or clipping the curb. On we drove, turning left and right, and suddenly I realised I was doing more than 30 miles per hour. *Oh Christ! Had he noticed? Of course he had. That's his job.* But there was nothing to be done now. I just had to concentrate on what I needed to do: an emergency stop. *Easy!* Finally, once we were back at the test centre, we stopped and so did my heart whilst I awaited the verdict.

"You have made two minor errors, but I am pleased to say you have passed your driving test."

Wow! Yes, yes, yes! At this very moment, my life was complete. The exams seemed like a lifetime away and my 17th birthday, along with its party tomorrow, seemed so unimportant. Never again in my life would I have to take a driving test. There may be many more academic exams, but this is something I would only need to do once and it was behind me.

That evening, I went out with my friends to celebrate the end of our exams and, of course, I was the driver. Being the second youngest in my year, there were others who could have passed their test, but only one other had. I was not going to miss the opportunity of being the driver on the first night of legal driving even if it did mean I would not be able to drink alcohol. Yes, I am still under age when it comes to drinking in a pub, but we all know it is possible. Anyway, I had a party arranged for Saturday night to celebrate my birthday, the end of my exams and, *now*, my having passed my driving test.

I drove around to Josh's house where he and David where waiting to be picked up. I was so proud as they got in and showered me with congratulations on passing my test.

"Waahay! Well done, Edmund," exclaimed Josh.

"Knew you would pass," added David.

Having parked, our legal drinkers went through the front door of the Catherine Wheel pub whilst a couple of us slipped around the back and waited till our friends came and sat at a table at the end of the beer garden. Now we could join a few other young people and, hopefully, not be noticed. I have been here a couple of times before and I'm never sure if the staff don't know we are under age or if they just don't want to know. Either way, a couple of hours drinking orange juice can get a little boring and all I really wanted to do was have the pleasure of driving us back

"Last orders!" came the call from the bar.

"Your round, I think," Helen said to David, and he duly got up and went to the bar.

When it had been my round, I had to give money to Mario who went to the bar for us all. Trying to get a group of not too sober young people out of a pub at closing time is no easy task, even for experienced bouncers – sorry – stewards. Eventually we were out and off to the Kebab House. Here was an unexpected problem. "Hey guys, please get lots of napkins to wipe your hands so you don't get grease all over my car."

They all did, but I'm sure I still got grease on my new pride and joy. First I had to drop Helen and her big brother, Mario, off at their house before taking Josh and David home. Then I was headed home for a very contented night's sleep. It had been a good day.

Saturday morning, I awoke to a noisy house. My parents and my younger brother and sister were preparing for their ten-week holiday in Australia. I was not going with them. Yes, I had been invited, but, as much as I wanted to see Australia, I think now was the time to stop going on family holidays and to start living my own life. I came out of my bedroom to see my mum dragging a large trunk. She dropped it, threw her arms around me and started to go through what she had said so many times before. "I will miss you, my darling boy, and I so wish you were coming with us."

I too would miss her, my father and both of my annoying little siblings, but a summer without my parents watching me would make it all worthwhile. In all fairness, they cannot be described as particularly controlling parents and have done everything possible to enable me to pass my driving test at the earliest possible date, but the thought of ten weeks doing whatever I wanted was more inviting than going to Australia. That could come later in life.

It was 7:30 pm and I arrived at the Minster Lovell village hall to help set up for the party. The DJ, Clive, was waiting to get in and set up and my friend, David, was also waiting to help me set up the tables and chairs. We virtually had them all set up when the caterers arrived. It was nothing very flash, but just enough for a simple meal for the 30 friends I had invited. I knew some may not turn up, but I also know there would be a few who would ask to bring a friend at the last minute. I just hoped the numbers would balance out. The meal was 8:30 pm for 9 p.m and as a few guests arrived, they helped the final set up. By now the music was playing, so already there was a party atmosphere. Soon after 9 pm the caterers started to serve us and by 10 pm we were moving the tables back so we could dance.

Not having a current girlfriend, I was hoping my luck might be in as there are a couple of girls in our year that I fancy. Jade knew I fancied her and was always friendly but never seemed to want to be anything more than friends. Serene may be a better bet, so I chatted her up. She was responsive but it might have been just because I was the host. I tried my luck once more with Jade and got the usual reaction. She was very flirtatious, but there was no follow-through. So I shifted my attention back to Serene. She was much more responsive this time, maybe because she had seen me dancing with Jade. I thought I was winning her favour, but by the end of the night, all I got was a kiss. There were tongues involved, yes, but she was clearly intent on leaving with her friends. By now Jade was also saying goodbye to her friends as her parents waited for her outside in the car. It seems I'd blown it! I played it far too long and tried to play one off against the other. My wonderful post exam experience had come to an end.

2

Computer Error

It was Sunday morning and I was the last to get up. The house was buzzing and at 9:30 am there was only one hour till my family would be leaving for two and a half months. Between snatching mouthfuls of breakfast cereal I helped to load the car. Soon it was 10:30 am and the hugs, kisses and long goodbyes began.

"Bye, son. Look after yourself."

"Yeah, bye, Dad. Have fun!" I replied as Dad slapped me on the back.

"Goodbye, my darling little boy."

"Bye-bye, Mum. I'll miss you." I struggled to free myself from her embrace.

As we live a 100 yards from a RAF base, there was a brief period of no talking as aircraft took off, but it only lasts about 30 seconds and it's not very often, so we hardly notice them now that we have got used to the occasional interruption to conversation. "Bye, Connor."

"Yeah, bye." He moved away.

"Oh, give your brother a hug, Connor; you won't see him for nearly three months."

"It doesn't matter, Mum." "Hey, Connor! Don't do anything I'd do. And if you do – don't get caught!" I said trying to lighten the situation.

"Pfft," Connor mumbled.

"Goodbye, my little sister."

"I'm not little!"

With that, they all got into the car. I didn't give a great deal of thought to their departure, really, as it felt like they were all off for a day out, but soon the car was disappearing down the drive and into the road amidst much waving and honking of the horn.

My mum is an Neuro Linguistic Practitioner, so a part of our house has always been used as a place of work where she would meet her patients. She says they are not "patients", but never seems too sure what word to use to describe them either. She usually calls them clients. When we were young, Mum would never have clients over outside of school hours, as she would need complete silence, but as we grew older, we have just had to learn to keep quiet when we are home and she is working. It's not easy, but she does have a separate room near the front door that she uses, so the rest of the house is okay. However, no music or shouting was allowed for half an hour or so. Mum says it's inconvenient, but it pays some of the bills and for some extras like my 17th birthday party. Dad is a pharmacist and owns a chemist in our small town. He has arranged for his chemist to be looked after by the manager for the ten weeks he is away. My sister, Lynsey, is 15 and in year 10 at the same school as me. She had no exams this year and was supposed to be in school for another few weeks, but is going to Australia anyway. Connor, my younger brother, is 13 and in year 8 at the same school, so really should also still be in school, but Australia is a once in a lifetime chance and he was not going to miss it and spend the last month at school just mucking about. I don't know if either of them got permission to take the time out of school, though. What irresponsible parents we have!

I went back into the house and got on with finishing breakfast and having a cup of tea. Suddenly it hit me that I was alone with nothing really planned and nothing much to do. I knew I'd have to look after myself for the 10 weeks and that was no problem, but the thought of not seeing my parents or my silly little brother and sister till September seemed an unbearably long time. I felt an immense sense of loss and abandonment. Our school is a semi boarding school and, although I am a day pupil, I remember at the beginning of year 7 how my friend, Josh, tried to explain how he felt when his parents had left him in a boarding school. His father is a diplomat in some far off place I can't pronounce – probably that place Borat comes from – and moves around a lot, so Josh has to be dumped in a boarding school. Josh had been 'dumped', but I had chosen to be left behind, so it's not quite the same, but now I do have a better idea of how he must have felt. The thought that I had another 83 years of hell to live through… What was I to do?

There was only one thing. It was now 10:57 am and in three minutes the first ball would be bowled in the first Ashes test. We don't have satellite television, as Mum and Dad are on a tight budget, so we always listen to the test match special online. I don't mind, really, as it is a 5-day event and if I sat in front of the television, I'd never get anything done, whereas listening to it is as exciting, but leaves me free to do other things. I opened the laptop and switched it on. There were 2 minutes to go and the screen saver came into view as the icons established themselves. Now there was only 1 minute left and just enough time to put in the web address and hear the voice of Jonathan Agnew. Who had won the toss? Would the winner choose to bat first or field first? It was brilliant sunshine here but what was the weather like where they were playing? If I were England's captain, I'd choose to bat first, get a good score on the board and then hope the skies cloud over tomorrow. The egg timer disappeared and it was exactly 11 am as I moved the pointer to the address bar and started typing 'bbc.co.uk/cricket'. I never bother with the 'www' bit. The computer's quite capable of putting that in. As I typed the 't' of 'cricket' the last 6 letters seemed to swirl around and become indecipherable. Was this a 'lysdexic' address bar? Clearly this was some sort of computer error. I noticed that I was now surrounded by the same sort of mist the last 6 letters were immersed in. I knew it was impossible, but the laptop appeared to lift off my lap, so I automatically grabbed it and pulled it down onto my lap again. Or that's what I thought. Although the laptop was once again on my lap, it seemed I was more attached to it than it attached to me. I was following it as it moved. What to do? Let go? Would that mean I would fall? Hang on and go with it? To where? Of course I hung on.

What felt like minutes was probably a few seconds. Bump! I felt as if I had fallen off my seat. The mist started to clear and the last 6 letters settled back into 'cricket'. My heart slowed and I asked myself if this had really happened. As my eyes lifted from the screen, I realised I was no longer sitting on the settee in my house but on the ground in a field. How could this be? Was I imagining this as well? I remained motionless as it dawned on me that I had moved through space. I was definitely no longer sitting on the settee in my house. My dad used to play an old Kinks song called 'Sitting on my sofa' and I longed to hear it and be there. I looked around. I was in a field! The field was pretty flat and I could see no people, but hundreds of sheep. In the distance was a church at least a mile away. I picked up the laptop and stood up. Now I could see a road about half a mile off leading to the church. Another road bisected it going what I thought was south by the position of the sun. There was no traffic on the road at all.

My desire to see where I was and to explore was taken over by the understanding that I was somewhere I had not chosen to come and needed to get back to where I was. But how? Obviously this had something to do with the computer error. I sat down again and looked at the keyboard. First I pressed the 'home' button. It seemed logical! Nothing happen. Then I moved the pointer to the address bar and thought hard about what to write. I tried 'home', 'reverse', 'back' and 'return'. Then I pressed the 7 key with the word 'home' on it. All to no avail. I looked at the screen and randomly began clicking all over it. I was not giving a lot of thought to what I was doing, but the mist began to return. Was I moving again? Would I go back or just go somewhere else? Would I go anywhere? Would I die? Once more the laptop began to lift and I knew what to do this time. I held on tight. This time I measured how long it took by counting. *1, 2, 3, 4...* Suddenly the mist began to clear again. Bump! I felt as if I had fallen off another chair. *Yes, yes, yes!* I was back in my house, sitting on my sofa. All praise be to Ray Davis. But how had I got back? I wasn't sure, but I think I clicked on the 'undo' button. That would make sense. I looked around and realised I was sitting just in front of the sofa I had been sitting on. So, yes, I had fallen off a seat. Perhaps I had been a little further forward when I came back than when I left, so I just missed the edge of the seat. That explained the bump when I went back. I had been sitting on a sofa at home but there was no seat in the field. Anyway, I was very relieved to be back in the security of my own home and my own world.

More to the point, never mind how I got back, where had I been and how did I get there in the first place? My mind was racing. Perhaps I had dreamt it all? I was pretty sure I had not. What had happened? How long was I gone for? I had no idea at all and felt a mixture of excitement and fear. I just had no idea at all how to make sense of it all. Of course it was impossible, but the fact was, it *had* happened. I had been to a different place that was completely empty except for hundreds of sheep. I had been filled with fear of never returning, yet had – by chance – found the way back. Perhaps I had not *found* a way back. Maybe I just returned by chance and it had nothing to do with my clicking on the 'undo' button or anything else to do with the computer. I had had a very lucky escape and I should be thankful for that.

3

Convalescence

I tried to fill my time with trivial activities such as reading the newspaper, watching television and making more and more tea. I could not even concentrate on the most important thing: the first Ashes test. Who had won the toss? Were the openers still in? How many runs had they got? How many were down? How many overs had been bowled? This helped me realise it was only 12:30 pm in the first session. Not much time had gone by when I take away the time I must have spent trying to do other things to take my mind off what had happened. Perhaps my time away was no time at all in the 'real' world. It might be like in a dream where a whole lifetime can be dreamed but only a few minutes of sleep have passed. Oh, how I wished my mum and dad were here. Even my little sister and brother would be welcome now. I knew I had to be with other people to take my mind off it and settle back to normality.

I picked up the 'phone to call Joe and began dialling, but switched it off as I knew I would not be able to speak. He was only half a mile away and I could cycle there in 3 minutes. Then it dawned on me that I had completely forgotten I had passed my test on Friday and could drive to him. I was so disturbed by my experience that I was forgetting who I was and what was going on in my life. Was

I becoming schizophrenic or psychotic? Certainly my assessment of reality was not what it should be. How could it be? I had just had an unreal experience. Or had I? I really did not know which was worst of all. I needed to get out but really didn't feel up to talking to people, so I decided to walk into town.

I turned on my special cricket radio I had bought last year at Edgbaston and slipped it over my ear. The man I had bought it from at the cricket ground had said it was a good fashion accessory and, although I like to think I am above such childish fashion needs, I had to admit I felt it looked cool. It was set to Radio 4's test match special and I heard Blowers' voice as I went to the door. It was now 12:55 pm and England were 92 for 1. Not a bad start. Or 1 for 92 as the Australian commentator now called it, which is only really confusing if a team loses wickets in the first over. It seemed ironic that I was listening to an Australian commentator's voice talking about the Australian team when my family were on their way to Australia. I got to the end of the drive and turned left towards the town as the phone rang. I answered it automatically and then remembered I didn't want to speak to anyone. It was too late now. It was Mum calling from Heathrow.

"Hello, Mum."

"Hello, darling. We're in the departure lounge. We just called for a final goodbye. I'll just pass you over to Dad"

"Hello, son."

"Hello, Dad."

"Bye! Here's Connor."

"Bye, Edmund."

"Yeah, bye, Connor."

In the background, I heard Mum say, "Come on, Lynsey."

"I've said goodbye to him!"

"Oh come on, Lynsey."

"No!"

I shouted down the phone, "It's all right, Mum. *Bye, Lynsey!*"

"Sorry, Edmund, she won't talk to you."

"It's all right, Mum. Bye then."

"Bye-bye, my darling, Edmund."

"Yeah, all right, bye, Mum," I said and switched the phone off.

To my surprise, I had found it quite easy to talk. Perhaps all I needed was a bit of normal life to bring me back to my senses.

By now, I was at the shops and decided to check my bank account to see how much Mum and Dad had deposited into my account to get me through the next 10 weeks. My balance was £1,065.32, so assumed they had put in £1,000 for me. It seemed a fortune, but knew if I was not careful, it would all go soon. Didn't really want to do the prodigal son bit to my parents. I withdrew £50, folded it and put it in my pocket. As I walked away from the ATM, I looked back at the Chinese take away next door and thought I'd probably be one of their best customers over the next few weeks. I looked at the flowers outside the greengrocer and then popped into Blockbusters to have a look around. I really didn't want anything and was just filling time. Then I walked around the corner and into the cycle shop. This seemed the natural thing to do as I often popped in there on a Saturday, but I had to remind myself again that my cycling days were almost over. Anyway, it filled a few more minutes and helped bring me back to normality; whatever that is, I can't be sure any more.

Next, I went over the road to the very useful shop and had a look around. I need a coaxial male to male connector for my friend's television but couldn't find one on display, so I had to ask. The assistant came over and had a look, but she too could only find a female to female connector. *Oh well, it's not a very useful shop,* I thought, so I went around the corner to the newspaper shop to buy a chocolate bar. It seems so long ago now, but it was only really a couple of years earlier I had been doing a paper round for this shop. I had not got off to good start, as I preferred the American idea of newspaper delivery – chucking it into the front garden. Pete, the shop owner, was most miffed and insisted the conventional method of actually putting it through the front door letter box was a better method of delivery. *Better for whom? Certainly not for a young teenager in a hurry.* Anyway, no sooner than I got used to this unreasonable expectation, my mum and dad made me give it up at the beginning of year 11. General Certificates of Secondary Education and all that, they said. Still, they did compensate me by giving me nearly as much pocket money as I had earnt delivering newspapers and I didn't have to get up at 5 am any longer.

By now, the second session of play was in full swing and England had moved on to 121 for 1. At this rate, they should get over 400. Then another wicket fell at 125. Now they were only heading for about 300. It was not nearly enough to give them something to bowl at when the Aussies were in.

I went to Dad's chemist shop before I remembered he would not be there, and as I stood looking across the road at St. John's Church, I remembered how, just a few years earlier, I was so bored I joined a Christian youth group and went through a religious stage just to be able to have something to do. They entice children into doing things like that. It reminds me of the man with sweeties at the school gate. How life has changed. Then I would not have believed that my computer would transport me to another place. I'm not too sure I believe it now. I walked back across the traffic lights and into the co-op. Mum had left me plenty of food, but I knew I needed some milk. I filled a bit more time looking around and then had a strange desire to buy some vintage cider as I'd heard it was very strong. It seems that cider has an image of not really being alcoholic like wine or beer, yet the alcohol content is much more than that of beer. Was just about to pick up a flagon when I remembered I would be asked for an ID, so it was a waste of time. Even though I felt much more grounded, I was clearly still not thinking properly. At least I saved myself the embarrassment of being challenged at the checkout and having to put it back. It's better to just get the milk and go home.

As I left, I heard a voice say, "Hello, Edmund!" It was Jenna's mum, Hermione, and she asked me the usual. I felt okay to chat now, but what could I say? Then she asked me, "How are you, Edmund?"

I thought about saying, 'Oh yes, Hermione, I've just been on a trip to a strange empty field surrounded by sheep and didn't know if I would ever get back again', but it was not likely she would believe me. The men in white coats would be here in no time. Even all the chemistry in Dad's shop couldn't cure that one. So I told her, "I'm fine, thank you. And yes, I will look after myself properly while they are all in Australia." I pre-empted her with a laugh. My family hadn't even left the country yet and already I have had the shock of my life.

"Oh good! Bye, Edmund."

"Bye, Hermione!"

It was time to walk home. I had thought that once I could drive, I would never walk again, but I needed the exercise and fresh air and felt much better for it. If I had driven, I would probably have crashed the car and would not have been able to explain to the police why I was incapable of driving along a straight road. As all children, I had been taught to always tell the truth. I don't think so! As I turned off the road and into our driveway, it did not seem the frightening place it had been a couple of hours earlier. Not only that, but England had moved on to 187 for 3.

I walked in through the back door and took my shoes off. Even when Mum is not there, I'm still conditioned. Anyway, I will have to clean the place before they get back, so I may as well try to keep it reasonably clean. I opened the fridge to put the milk in and took out some coleslaw, a packet of bread rolls and some spread. I got a plate out of the cupboard and made myself a coleslaw sandwich. Then I ate it, drank some orange juice and put the dirty stuff in the dishwasher. Without thinking, I walked into the sitting room and looked at the settee. There was my laptop. It seemed to be calling me to open it and got back to where I had been before. I felt like Gollum being called by the ring. Was I being taken over? Would I be able to resist?

In the background, I heard, "197 for 3."

4

Cuddles in the Kitchen

I closed my laptop and put it away in my bedroom. Mum was always telling me to put it away and not just leave it lying around, and now I was doing it to avoid being continually reminded of what I *think* had happened and what I might feel the need to do in the future. What was I going to do with the rest of my day? Nothing had been arranged, but I knew a night out could be sorted with a phone call.

My mobile rang and I looked at the caller's name. It was Serene. I answered with excitement. "Hello, Serene!"

"Hello, Edmund. How you doing?"

"Fine, thanks. You?"

"Yes, me too."

A long pause followed as I tried to think of what to say. Clearly we were both finding it difficult to talk to each other, which was strange as we never had that problem at school.

"Er, Edmund, I was wondering if you liked bowling."

"Well…" There was a roar in the background and I realised Strauss had got his century. "Yes! Yes! Yes! Strauss has got a century. Whoopee!" My excitement seemed to dispel my nerves and I talked over Serene saying, "Oh, you're not a cricket fan, are you? Yes, I'd love to go bowling with you." It suddenly occurred to me this was a little presumptuous as she hadn't actually asked me and she may be suggesting a gang of us go bowling. Anyway, it was too late now.

"Oh great! Can you make it tonight?"

"Yes, of course. Shall I pick you up at 8pm?" For years I had wanted to be able to say I'd pick a girl up in *my* car, rather than being driven around by my parents, or somebody else's, and now I was loving the dream.

"Oh no, Edmund, I only live just around the corner! I'll see you outside at 8pm."

"Okay. If that is all right with you I'll see you there and then."

"Cool. Bye till then, then."

"Yes. Bye, Serene."

Oh well. I'll have to wait for another opportunity to say, *"pick you up at eight and don't be late!"*

What excitement! All thoughts of computer errors evaporated and I rushed upstairs to have a shower. How things had changed. There were no more worries of psychosis. As I was getting out of the shower, play closed with England on 284 for 4. It was not a bad day's play.

As I was drying myself and still feeling positive, I made the inevitable decision – I had to go back to wherever it was at some time. What else could I do? I'd never know for sure if I didn't, and I wanted to know for sure and find out where it was. From the number of sheep, it could be Australia. Did I get transported to where the rest of my family were flying? It looked too green for Australia, but it is their winter season and it is a big place. Actually, I had no idea at all where it was and that was the main reason I had to go and check. I wanted to tell Serene but where would I start? I expect that would put her off completely. How could I start to explain, but I really need to share this with someone. I would have to see how the evening goes.

I left in plenty of time to park and be outside by 8 pm and at 7:55 pm I approached the entrance to Hollywood Bowls. There was Serene waiting and looking very attractive in a knee length dress that was clinging to her figure. I parked as quickly as possible and tried not to run to her so as I casually walked up and said 'hello', I leant forward to kiss her mouth. I was pleased by her response and we walked in. I hadn't been here in years and had no idea how much everything had changed. As we discussed how many games we should play Serene pushed a tenner into my hand and asked me to book two games. I paid and found we had a few minutes to wait. As we sat chatting, she didn't seem like the girl I had spent six years at school with. That girl was a mate and just another school girl. This Serene was a gorgeous young lady. She had looked attractive at my party but now – *wow*! I couldn't tell if that was because she really did look better or if I viewed her differently now that I was on a date with her. It didn't really matter, as I felt she also liked me.

When the game started, I got off to a good start and Serene got off to a bad one. Should I try to beat her or make her feel good by losing? Would that be patronising? I did not have long to think about it before getting a foul for overstepping the line and Serene got a spare. Now we were about even. My competitive nature took over and I went for a win. The best laid schemes of mice and men often go awry! 5 minute later the game was over and I had lost. Oh well, one game left. Off we went I was soon in the lead. Serene got a couple of noughts and I got two strikes, so not only did I win, but I scored nearly twice as much as in my first game. It felt good and Serene didn't seem to mind. When she had asked for two games, I thought about what would happen if we each won a game and there is no winner, but now I realised it was better this way as no one looked like a loser. Honours were shared and I had had no need to patronisingly lose to her. Or perhaps she *had* patronised me by losing? Who cares?

Without thinking, we had a very natural cuddle at the end of the game and then there was a pregnant pause. *What now?* I stumbled over my words and asked, "How about a drink?"

"Sure," she said and we walked over to the bar. There were signs all over the place saying that it was a bar for over 21 only and I knew neither of us would get away with it, so ordered two orange juices. At least there was no loss of face at being too young as we were both in the same boat, but I couldn't help but feel I looked like a schoolboy and Serene looked like a sophisticated young lady. Still, she didn't seem to have a problem with it, so we sat and chatted. After a while, the nerves of our first date seemed to disappear and we both chatted as if we were still at school. I can't really remember what was said, but it was mostly insignificant stuff. That didn't matter, as I was constantly thinking that I had an empty house at home but didn't know how to raise the issue. We chatted on and our glasses were empty as it approached 9:30 pm There was a short silence and I asked, "Would you like another drink?"

"Okay," she said.

As I got up, I blurted out, completely out of context, "Would you like to come back for coffee?" I believe that amongst university students that is a euphemism for 'would you like to come back for sex'. Serene just looked at me for what seemed like a whole minute. I started to mumble, "Er, later... If you want to. I mean, you don't have to, I just thought..." I was digging myself in deeper. Why couldn't I just shut up?

Serene looked me straight in the eye and said, "Okay, but I need to be home by 11 p.m. or 11:30 pm at the latest." *Oh my God! What was she saying?* Once more I started to mumble, but then got control of myself and said rather quietly and sheepishly, "Well, perhaps we had better leave now." Serene just picked up her jacket and stood up. *Keep calm, keep calm, keep calm! Don't let her think you are desperate or counting your chickens.* I couldn't believe it, but managed to prevent myself from clicking my heels.

We walked out a lot faster than we had walked in and got into my car. As Serene had walked to the bowling alley, because she didn't live far from it, I needed to get her back here later. I tried to drive home slowly, calmly and serenely, but the only sort of serene I could think of, was the one sitting next to me. We hardly spoke as we drove, but what was there to say? Eventually we turned into the driveway and I parked the car. We walked around the back and into the kitchen. I felt the need to go through the motions and put the kettle on as I asked Serene how she liked her coffee.

"One sugar and lots of milk," she said quickly.

As I stirred the coffee, I turned around to find Serene standing close behind me. I wasn't sure what to do, so I put my arms around her and squeezed her as she responded. I will always remember our cuddles in the kitchen to get things off the ground. We kissed and I disentangled myself as I picked up both cups and said, "Come on." I was pushing my luck here a bit but it was no problem as she followed me upstairs.

At 11:05 pm we left our driveway and headed towards her home and a quarter of an hour later I stopped at the end of her road before giving her a quick goodbye kiss. It wasn't really late, so I don't think her parents will ban me from seeing her again. Apart from anything else, they have known me for 6 years now. As I turned into my driveway, I had a great sense of tranquillity. What a turn around from a few hours ago. I had wanted to tell Serene about my little adventure but had not known how to raise the matter. Anyway, I have to admit, I had better things to talk about and do. If I went again and *did* return, I could always tell her next time.

I walked into the house and went straight to bed, but could not go to sleep straight away as I thought about what adventures awaited me tomorrow. Should I go back there and walk around? Should I take something to drink? Something to eat? How long would I be there? Should I have a test run and just go there and come back to make sure I can? Next time I must check the time before I go and when I come back to see how 'real time' relates to dream time'. From the fact that I plopped onto the ground when I arrived, and missed the settee when I returned, I guess there's a direct correlation between a position here and a position there. I can't believe I'm talking like this. There? Where is 'there'? I still wasn't too sure if 'there' actually existed. What if I couldn't come back? What would my family think had happened to me? There would be no trace. If I could not get back, would that be because I was dead or because I was alive elsewhere? Which would be worst for me? Either way, it would make no difference to my family as they wouldn't know. Was I being selfish? Definitely, but what is adolescence for? I knew that by this time tomorrow I would know and eventually drifted off to sleep.

5

Another Time

As I awoke, I immediately became completely conscious and fully aware of what I had resolved to do today. My eyes sprung open and focussed on the clock. It was 7:09 am I got out of bed and dressed much quicker than when I have to go to school. Mum had made me promise I would not just get out of bed and leave it unmade for ten weeks, and as this was just the first day of ten weeks, I didn't feel I was breaking any promise by leaving it unmade. I went downstairs and immediately picked up my laptop. Then I paused. I needed to slow down. I must do this slowly, calmly and make sure I don't forget anything. I had given a lot of thought to how I would do things this time, but still wasn't sure about some aspects of how to play it. Mainly I was wondering whether I should go and then immediately return just to check if it worked. I tried to calm down and leisurely had a big breakfast of cereal followed by three pieces of toast. After all, I didn't know when I would be eating again or when I was coming back – if ever! As these thoughts ran through my head. I switched the laptop on, logged on and opened Internet Explorer.

Having breakfasted, I cleaned my teeth and prepared a litre bottle of squash to take with me. I also remembered to get out my laptop case so I could easily carry around the computer if I needed to. Having worked out that space was similar in the other place, I knew it was important to come back to exactly the same spot or I may have some extreme difficulties. For example, six feet further forward would put me in the middle of the house wall. It's probably best to avoid that! I really was very frightened of what might happen. Not so much for myself, but for my mum, dad and younger siblings who would never have the faintest idea of what had happened. Now, of course, there was an extra person to consider: Serene. I wanted to tell her last night, but how would I have started? The truth was, I was so involved in the here and now of last night I hardly gave any thought to what I had planned the next day. Now I wish I had said at least something in case I never see her again. But what? Should I have mumbled something like 'if you never see me again, don't take it personally' and hope she didn't ask any questions? That was just silly. Eventually I consoled myself with the thought that if I had said anything, things would not have panned out as they had.

I was all ready: clean and tidy with the laptop case and a bottle of squash. I had combed my hair whilst thinking how I probably had my priorities wrong in wanting to look good when I had no idea what I was entering into. Suddenly I realised I'd nearly forgotten something vital. I rushed into the garden and looked around for Linsey's old plastic windmill. She was far too old for it now, but had planted it in the garden years ago where I hoped it would still be. Not in the back garden, around the front, and there it was, sticking out of one of the flower beds. It was a bright blue windmill on a white stick and would be perfect for marking any spot I had arrived at so that I could come back to exactly the same spot and avoid that wall. Then I loaded the dishwasher with my breakfast things and started tidying up the kitchen, realising that I was making excuses not to get on with it. I needed to gather my resolve and apply myself to what I had to do. I dried my hands, took the bottle of squash out of the fridge, took a deep breath and walked into the sitting room where the laptop was on the sofa waiting for me. It really did feel as if it *was waiting for me*! As if it had been calling for me to return to the other place. As if I were its tool, not it mine.

Eventually I sat on the sofa and placed the laptop case on my lap, followed by the laptop with the windmill and bottle of squash tucked in between the laptop and my tummy. My hands were shaking as I moved the pointer to the address bar and began to type in the URL 'bbc.co.uk/cricke…'. At that point, I paused to look at the clock so that I could check my time away. The clock on the DVD read 8:37 am and I checked my watch to see if it correlated. It did. I looked at the keyboard and sucked in as much air as I could hold in my lungs as my shaking finger touched the last letter of the website address – 't'. My hands grasped the laptop as I saw the last six letters of the address swirling. It *was* happening again. The mist spread and was all around me now as I was counting my time of 'travel': *4, 5, 6, 7… 19, 20, 21…* Bump! I knew I had landed again and looked around. It seemed like the same place: An empty field, except for hundreds of sheep. I looked at them and they looked at me. They didn't seem to be surprised to see me and I had to remind myself that sheep are not known for their powers of wonderment. Looking at my watch to check the time. I was pleased to see it was only 8:38 am It seemed time was not bending – even if space was. As I stood up, I was overwhelmed by fear and immediately sat down again and moved the pointer to 'undo' and clicked it. The mist swirled and I counted: *3, 4, 5… 20, 21…* Bump! I was back home. The mist cleared and I looked around just to check it was my sitting room. It was, and this time I was sitting on the sofa with my legs half on and half off it. Not comfortable, but successful. As I slipped my legs to the floor, I looked at the DVD clock to see 8:38 a.m. My watch said the same. Time in the other place was the same as time here, even if I had no idea where the other place was. My fear disappeared immediately. It seemed the travelling was controllable.

What now? Should I thank my lucky stars that I could return and just be satisfied with what I had discovered? That would be the sensible thing but I was never praised at school, or by my parents, for being sensible. This time, with more of a sense of excitement rather than trepidation, I moved the pointer to the address bar and started typing 'bbc.co.uk/cricke...'. I stopped, not out of fear but just to look at the clock. It read 8:40 a.m. I pressed the last key – 't'. Once more the letters swirled and the mist spread all around me as I counted. *4, 5, 6... 18, 19, 20, 21...* Bump! I was back in the same place with the same sheep. Well, I think they were the same sheep but I'll have to admit, they all look the same to me. It was clearly the same place, but it felt like a different world. I felt no fear; just excitement and anticipation.

I put the laptop on the ground with the windmill and the bottle next to it and opened the case. Then I picked up the laptop and put in it inside the case and zipped it up. Now to pick up the windmill and stick it in the ground where I had been sitting. I had one last look around and by the position of the sun I tried to establish north, south, east and west. But was it 8:41 am in the other place? The sun was low in the sky, so it seemed quite early in the day, but was it summer? If it were midwinter, the sun would be low any time. It was quite warm for early morning and I could see a few chewed bushes and they were in full leaf, so I assumed it was summer. I thought this must have been what the South Downs looked like before they stopped sheep farming in that part of the country and it all became scrub. I had read about how terrible it was that that this type of countryside was being lost because of the change in farming. I couldn't see how the bare fields were better, but who am I to judge? I wondered if this was the Sussex Weald. There were fields to the north but nothing really to the south. It was pointless wondering really. It could be absolutely anywhere in the world. *Or* maybe another world?

Once more I looked towards the church in the distance I had seen the first time and it appeared to be to my east. As it was the only land mark I could see, it seemed logical to head towards it. Off I strode and thought it looked about a mile away, so I expected to get there in about 20 minutes if I didn't hang about. Before I got there, I arrived at the road I had seen the first time and found it wasn't a proper road but just a mud track. When I say mud, it's actually more dust than mud. I looked to the north and could see the other road crossing it was also only a track, but it did seem to be heading towards the church, so I walked towards the junction. Then it struck me that even if it was only a mud track, there was no traffic around; vehicular or human. At the crossroads, I turned east towards the church and took a swig of squash.

Up ahead I could see a man in the distance just before the church, so I assumed I could get some information as to where I was. I sped up in case he walked off the other way. He didn't move at all, except to lean against a tree, and watched me as I approached. He was on the side of the road and surrounded by sheep. When I got close enough to see his garb, it struck me as strange. By now his gaze was changing into a stare and I could see his clothes were not made of summer cotton, but some rough looking material which was torn and very dirty. His jaw dropped as I got closer. *Hadn't he seen a clean man before?* I was now a few feet away and realised the smell of the sheep was being greatly added to by his personal smell. He continued to stare and I said, "Hello?" He continued to stare and said nothing, so I asked, "Could you tell me where I am?"

His mouth moved but nothing came out. Eventually he made some sounds, but nothing I could understand. I repeated, "Could you tell me where I am?"

The man spoke again and I realised he was not speaking English. Was this man a foreigner, perhaps, or was I in a foreign country where I was the foreigner? "Sorry, could you say that again?"

Silence. Then, once again, his jaw moved but nothing came out. I stood there, looking and feeling confused, embarrassed and uncomfortable. Once more he spoke, and I thought I recognised a few sounds. It reminded me of Chaucer's work, which made me smile. I had loved studying Chaucer for English AS and enjoyed seeing how the language had changed from a form of German/Dutch/Frisian to what we now call English. Shakespearian English is just about intelligible to our ears, but two hundred years before Shakespeare, Chaucer's language was drastically different and meaningless to most people in the 21st century. Was this man German? Was I in Germany? I had learnt a little German in school, so asked him the same question in German. He continued to stare and spoke again. This time I thought I recognised a few sounds and once more was struck by how much it sounded like Chaucer's English. It was worth a try! I put my question in what I thought would sound like 14th century English. His face relaxed a bit and he said something that sounded like St. Petter. Petters? Petter? Better? *What's better? Britus?* Then I asked, "St. Britus?"

The man gave a vague nod. St. Britus? St. Britus? *St. Britius!* Was he saying St. Britius? The name of our only old church in the area? This church should be about a mile from where I live, but *my* church was a lot older looking than this church. However, as I turned to look at the church, I thought it did look very similar to that church, apart from it not being nearly as old. I'd not studied the church before and only ever drove past it, but it did look very similar. The road I was on ran along side it and there was another road at the T-junction that ran down the other side of the church. I looked at the man and asked again,"St. Britius?"

The man nodded. Looking at him again, I couldn't help but think he didn't look very healthy. I'm not surprised considering all that dirt. I took a step towards him and he stepped back. *It's not me that's stinking*, I thought. Then I asked, "Brize Norton?"

He shrugged and said, "St. Petter."

He must be saying Britius, just with a different accent. This is the only church in the country dedicated to St. Britius, so it couldn't be any other church. But where was Brize Norton, the village around the church? It's not a big village, but a village nevertheless. There was nothing here except a couple of shabby sheds a few hundred yards away. Then I noticed a more substantial building in the distance behind the man. Was this St. Britius in Brize Norton? What else could it be?

The man still stood there and stared in a way that was not very subtle, looking me up and down. I did not return the insult. At this point, he looked over my shoulder and I turned around to see what had caught his eye. A man in long black clothes was standing by the church. A monk or a priest? Perhaps the church vicar? He looked a lot cleaner and I thought I'd get further talking to him, so as I walked towards him, I called out, "Excuse me!"

When I got closer, he stepped back as the other man had done. I had learnt that in very sparsely populated places personal space is much greater than it is in crowded cities, and assumed this was the reason why they had both stepped back as I got close. I said, "Sorry to trouble you, but is this St. Britius' Church?"

The vicar looked at me blankly and once more I tried the same question in what I thought to be Chaucerian English. The vicar answered in the same strange tones and I'm sure he was saying that it was. Then he said something like, "Where are you from, sir?"

Oh my God! What was I to say? This was not *my* St. Britius, so how could I say I come from over there, a mile back. If he was the local vicar and the population was that small, he would know me or at least know there was not a house over there. Thinking quickly I said, in my best medieval English, that I came from a far off land. This seemed to satisfy the priest and I realised we were able to have a conversation even if things were not perfect. As I had said I came from a far off land, this was enough for him to accept my strangeness of using his language. He ushered me into his church and I followed him in somewhat reluctantly. What else could I do? I could hardly run off. Although I was reluctant, I did want to continue to find out more about this place.

Inside, the vicar offered me a drink of water from a rough mug and I accepted it to be polite. We began to chat and he seemed to be happy to tell me about the place. After all, I was a stranger in his land and he probably wanted to tell me about his world as he knew I was a 'foreigner'. Having told me the local people were very rich, I thought about the man in the dirty, torn, rough clothing. *If they were rich, what did the poor look like?* This priest was relatively clean, but his hands were not very clean and neither were his finger nails. I think he said something about the plague and I asked for more detail. He looked confused and said, "It landed in the south a few weeks ago." What was this? A different strain of flu? Smallpox? Cholera? Oh no, cholera was caught from dirty water and could not be described as a plague. He went on to talk about the spread of the disease and the speed at which its victims died, and how he felt for the people and especially his fellow priests who seemed to be disproportionately stricken by the illness. He kept repeating how he prayed to God for deliverance and that he was sure the good Lord would save the children of his holy church. By children I assumed he meant Christians and not children as in young people. He was clearly frightened of the plague but I had no idea what he was referring to.

As he was talking, I thought. The plague that landed in the south, Chaucerian English... Oh no! Was he referring to the Black Death? St. Britius, the rough roads, the lack of buildings? Was I where I lived but not in the same period? In the same place but not the same time? Had I got three dimensions right and the crucial forth one wrong? Was I in medieval England? In the 14th century? I became aware that I was gawking and the priest had gone quiet. He asked, "Did you not know?"

I said something about knowing but not realising the severity of the situation. Now I understood why he and the other man had stepped away from me as I approached. So why had this priest asked me into his church? Probably out of Christian kindness and because I looked foreign and a lot cleaner than the locals. Maybe another reason was that in a strictly organised social structure I was high in rank as I was clean, well dressed, even if it's rather strangely, probably educated and I had the confidence of the upper echelons of society. Things were falling into place as I understood what was happening, but the gravity of the realisation that I was in a different time began to dawn on me.

The priest offered me some more water and I instinctively said, "No, have some of mine." I picked up the bottle I had put on the floor and proffered it. Realising I was offering a plastic bottle, I withdrew my hand but the priest's eye had caught the bottle and he raised his mug. I removed the top, now remembering it was orange squash, and poured some into his mug. The priest raised it to his mouth, sniffed and sipped.

"Mmm! Beautiful, is it a honey concoction?"

"Yes," I said, thankful for the way out.

Then he said, "That is a strange bottle, sir. May I look at it?"

Tentatively, I passed over the bottle which he took and studied. Excuses ran through my brain and eventually he asked, "What is it made from?"

"It's a leather material, dried in a special way that makes it look like that."

"Mmm... May I?" he asked, touching the top.

He had obviously seen me open it and twisted the top off himself as I nodded. "Ingenious!" he said and handed me back the bottle. I had survived another awkward situation.

The priest's body language indicated he wanted to end the conversation. Maybe he was bored or maybe he had other things to do. Either way, I was pleased to have the opportunity to get away and rose to my feet. I offered my hand and remembered physical contact was a no-no in times of plague. He flinched a little and shook my hand. I was now wondering if hand shaking was a social ritual in medieval times. I think it had been a Roman thing, so probably yes. Anyway, it indicated my equality with a priest, so I was not regarded as a peasant like that poor man outside. This made me ask, "Who is the peasant outside?"

"Ah, him. He's not a peasant: he's a surf to Monks in Black Bourton called Edric." I knew the doomsday book had used the words 'surf' and 'slave' interchangeably, so I had an idea of his status and that he had no right to anything, including his clothes that were the responsibility of the church. He had the responsibility of working for the priory. I could see who was getting the better side of the deal. Little has changed! All doubts that this was where I lived, only in a different time, were now dispelled. Black Bourton is still a little village about 2 miles from Brize Norton.

"Thank you for your hospitality," I said as the priest raised his hand and blessed me.

I was not sure how to respond to this not being religious, let alone Catholic, which of course everybody was in the 14th century. After all, that is what the word Catholic means. I gave a little bow and made my way towards the door. I was tempted to ask him what the date was, but knew this would be pointless as the calendar has changed since then and the answer would be rather meaningless. However, I had studied medieval history along with Chaucer and knew the Black Death had landed in the south in 1348, having spread from somewhere around the Russian steppes only a few years earlier. It was probably brought to England on a ship. This was the main way in which it had made its way west over the previous few years.

Once outside, I had another look around and waved to Edric who was now staring at me again. The priest had probably wanted to do the same, but he had more social graces than poor Edric. I stared back at him. *Never mind, mate. Even if this plague does get you, it will hasten the end of this terrible socio-economic system. The transition to capitalism will not be smooth or easy but, even if capitalism is far from perfect, it has to be better than what gives you this life.* I would have liked to have had a conversation with him about the Marxist concept of the process of history, but felt that even if we could understand each other perfectly, he would not have the faintest idea of what I was talking about. Neither would I had it not been for my mother's years of telling me we only live in a period of history known as capitalism, but that there is nothing permanent about it. With this thought I turned and walked east towards the crossroads.

As I walked, my head was racing. How had this happened? Had it happened at all or was I still in a very long dream? Either way, I had to deal with it as a reality. It reminded me of the philosophy concept of phenomenology. Whether or not the table is still there when I do not perceive it, if I perceive it by banging my leg against it, it will still hurt, so I have to accept this world as if it *is* real. Walking back I looked at my surroundings differently from when I was walking to St. Britius.

As I approached the Carterton crossroads, I was thinking that for another 700 years into the future this scene would not change much at all. There were no houses here and the land would still be used for grazing sheep. What else can one do with marginal land? Until other forms of employment emerged in later years, there was no choice other than to farm in a subsistence manner. So, standing at the crossroads I stopped and looked around. There was no co-op, no pub, no Blockbuster and no estate agents. Oh well, not all things are better than they been in the middle ages!

Down the road towards Black Bourton and a few hundred yards further on I stopped and looked into the distance towards Black Bourton, thinking how, as of the 1950s, no one would be able to walk through to Black Bourton because the Americans closed that road to extend the air base when they held the Brize Norton air base post World War II. What would Edric and the priest think? Not a lot probably, as it would be hundreds of years after their deaths.

I turned right off the road and crossed the field towards the point I thought should be about the beginning of what would be Milestone road. I looked around for the milestone and could not see one, so I assumed that it was put there years after the period I was in now. I walked on and soon picked up the sight of the blue windmill blades. I had guessed well and approached the place as fast as I could. Nothing had gone wrong, and nothing had frightened me, so why the hurry? It was probably just because I was in an unbelievable situation; in another time. I needed to get back to a sense of security. As I reached the blue windmill, I picked it up and tried to sit exactly where I had placed it. I opened the laptop case and put the computer on my lap. I had left it in hibernation mode so had to wait for it to come back to life. When it had, my finger moved towards the 'undo' button and I clicked it with a slight sense of fear but more with a warm sense of a homecoming and security. The letters in the address bar swirled and the mist spread all around me as it had done before. I don't know if it was forgetfulness because my head was full of what had happened, or faith that it would work, but I did not count this time. No sooner than the mist had started swirling it began to clear again.

6

Burford

"Burford! Burford! My Lord Burford!"

"Lechlade, what is all the excitement?"

"The king has news of the plague. The word is it has reached Clanfield."

"Oh, dear Lord. It must have been brought down the Thames and landed at Radcot."

"Or up the road from the south coast?"

"Yes, that's possible. Has the Earl of Gloucester been informed?"

"I don't know, but I expect word reached him before it reached us here at Windsor."

"I am just back from collecting my younger son, Stephen, from school in London, but I must return to Burford to be with my household and rally the people. Where is my elder son, Henry?"

"I do not know but believe he is still within the castle."

Burford dismounted and called to a servant, "You, man, find my son Henry, and tell him to prepare to return to Burford."

"Yes, My Lord."

"Are you going back to Lechlade?"

"Yes, we are already packed and ready to leave. This may be the last we see of each other for a while as we will all have to stay in our homes till the plague passes."

"You are right. Give my blessings to your wife and family and tell them we shall meet for a celebratory meal once this horror has passed."

"I certainly will, Burford. Give my felicitation to your family and may the Lord be with you all. Good day and good luck."

"Good day, Lechlade, and may the Lord be with you also."

"Scabbard!" Burford called to his manservant who was continuing to unload the boat on the river that had just brought them back from London downstream. "Stop unloading the boat. We must gather all our belongings and reload the boat, plus another two, and return to Burford. Everything must be gathered as we do not know how long it will be before we are in Windsor again. I must see the king and beg his leave."

The herald announced, "The Lord Burford."

Burford entered and genuflected before the king.

"My Liege, I beg your leave to return to my family and the people of Burford to prepare for the arrival of the plague."

"Of course, My Lord, and please feel free to take anything you or the people of Burford may need in these terrible times."

"Thank you, Sire, we will need some food for our journey. I shall instruct Scabbard to visit the kitchens before we leave."

"I wish you Godspeed and may he watch over us all."

"Thank you, Sire. I remain your true and trusted servant." Burford walked backwards and turned to leave the royal chambers.

Two hours later the boats were loaded and ready to leave. All three boats were low in the water being laden with belongings, provisions and people. It was now an hour past noon and progress was fast as the convoy made its way upstream through Maidenhead. Here it was necessary to land as they made progressed through the rocks under Cleavedon toward Merlow. As it was necessary to land again, this was a good place to spend the night, but it was still light and the cox thought the party could make Henley before midnight, so they pressed on. Time was important as families may be distraught awaiting the arrival of their loved ones and because the people of Burford needed to be rallied to the challenge as soon as possible.

By the time Henley was in sight, it was completely dark but the party landed and made its way into the town to find a bed for the night. Henley, being full of inns, provided a good choice for the discerning traveller, but quality was not the main decider, so the first inn was adequate for the Burfords and a few others whilst the rest of the party found rooms further up the town. A quick meal was requested and questions asked as to the plague's progress. The inn landlord said, "Yes, the people have heard of the sickness upstream, but there is no evidence of it in Henley, though the people, especially the lower orders, are very frightened." The inn landlord told Lord Burford that many of the lower orders still worshipped the pagan Gods, so they had more to fears as they would not have the protection of the one true Church of God. It was no surprise to hear that many had recently become baptised into the Church of Rome.

Lord Burford agreed with the landlord and opined, "This may protect them and, even if they were to die, at least they would know their souls were saved and they would live forever in the Lord Jesus Christ." In normal times, there would have been much merrymaking and quaffing of ale, but these were not normal times, so once everybody had eaten, it was off to bed for a good sleep before rising to continue the journey home.

Soon after dawn, the Burford family were breaking their fast and gathering their belongings before messengers were sent around the town to ensure all were at the boats as soon as possible. It was another bright morning as Lord Burford walked to the boats and boarded. There was a little early morning mist but the sun was quickly burning it off and the floodplain and surrounding hills looked beautiful in the early morning sunlight. Asking if all were there, he was informed that only two were still in the town but would be there soon. Five minutes later the laggards arrived, giving their excuses, and the three boats moved off upstream.

Having negotiated various rocks and shallows that forced them to land again, the party approached Abingdon by early evening. Now a similar decision to the previous night was necessary. Should they stop for the night or press on to Oxford for the night? Lord Burford decided that it would be better to land and rest at Abingdon to be able to rise early and reach Burford the next day. Soon the boats were alongside the steps and, boat by boat, the crews unloaded to go into the town to find lodgings for the night. Once more the party was split between more than one inn, and some requested of their lord to be allowed to make merry. Permission was granted, but only on the proviso that *all* were aboard again by the time it began to get light the next morning. Lord Burford was aware of the times ahead and that this may be the last night the crew may have to relax for a long time.

In the town the inn keepers and others were questioned about the progress of the disease, but there was no real evidence that it had progressed further or even that it definitely was in Clanfield now. That village was only 20 miles further up stream, but it seemed that over the last couple of days there had been a flood of people out of the area. All claimed, however, they were merely passing through and did not come from any plagued village. What else could they say? All travellers downstream were treated with suspicion and anyone who said they had been in Clanfield or Radcot, would have been forced out. As for those going upstream, there were very few, but those who were all had family reasons to do so, like Burford and his party. There were even inns that said they were running out of provisions because the flow of food around the area was being cut drastically, as most traders were staying in their homes and villages to try to avoid contact with strangers. However, enough food could be found for those with the money to pay for it, like Lord Burford. This was eaten, ale was drunk and bed was taken early for an early rise.

As the skies began to lighten, Scabbard approached his lord and told him that all were ready at the river. It was only a few yards from the inn, and five minutes later the first boat was pushing off from the bottom of the steps. The final leg of the journey had begun and the convoy was soon passing through Oxford were the 19-year-old Henry Burford had been studying at Balliol College for the last 2 years. It was unlikely he would be returning this autumn, as all colleges were expected to close until the pestilence had passed. There was much bustle on the riverside and most traffic was going downstream. Oxford, being a large city, was already draining of people running for the supposed safety of the countryside as the plague was expected to arrive any moment. At Eynsham, the party stopped to eat and rest and a man was dispatched to hire a horse and ride to Beamtune Castle to request horses and carts to meet them at Tadpole. Had they been travelling in smaller boats, they would have gone up the Windrush river as it flows into the Thames at Standlake. The Windrush also flows through Burford and straight past Burford House where the Burford family resides.

By early evening, the first boat rounded the bend to see men and horses waiting for them. Steam was rising from the horses, so it was clear they had not long arrived. The baggage and the rest of the party could now be left for Scabbard to bring on to Burford, whilst Lord Burford and his two sons, Henry and Stephen, rode on to Burford as fast as possible. Within minutes, all three were astride their horses and heading towards Chimney on their way to Beamtune. The fields on either side of the road were virtually flat and full of barley waiting to be harvested. This showed the four-year farming cycle was in its third year and the next year would be fallow. Lord Burford looked at them and said to his sons, "It is just as well the next year will be fallow as no planting may be done next spring anyway."

Henry replied, "Let's hope they can find the men fit and willing to harvest this year's crop before it rots in the field or we shall all starve."

On they galloped and as they approached Beamtune, they could hear the bustle of the market. As they rode into the village, they found it full of people but there were many empty places where stalls would normally be set up. What stalls there were seemed empty and it became clear that traders were afraid to come to Beamtune and the local people were buying all they could to stock up for an unknown period until the disease passed. There was a sense of panic in the air. After all, Clanfield was only two or three miles further on from Beamtune.

The three of them rode up to the castle gates and Sir Richard was waiting for them. "Good day, My Lord Burford, Henry, Stephen. I hope you are well. You are very well come despite the imminent problems."

"We are well, Sir Richard," replied Lord Burford, "but even if we are well come, we cannot stay as we must return to our family as soon as possible and prepare the town for the arrival of the plague."

"I understand, My Lord, but can you not just stop for a drink?"

"We can, sir, and you can tell me about the progress of the disease."

The Burfords dismounted and food and drink was produced as Sir Richard told them what he knew. "A man was showing the unquestionable signs of the plague five days ago, and is now boarded up in his home with his family. His door has been painted with a cross and food is being left by a window for them. He may well be dead by now. We do not know what has become of him or his family. The man works at the wharf in Radcot and is suspected to have caught the disease from someone who stopped on the river at Radcot. Whether that man went on downstream or took the road is not known. There is no sign of the disease in Farringdon yet, so it is unlikely it came from Southampton and Wight up the road. There is much panic abroad, but preparations are being made and special masses are being held in the churches. I have ordered the Clanfield Road to be blocked and no one is allowed into the town from the west."

After the food and drink has been consumed, the Burfords remounted and as they were about to leave, one of Sir Richard's men ran up, shouting, "A woman has fainted in the market and cannot get up again!"

"Tell us more," said Sir Richard.

"Well, little more is known as the woman is lying in the road and no one will touch her."

"It could be the plague or she may just be ailing from the fear of what is to come," said Lord Burford.

"I shall send a woman to wash her in vinegar," said Sir Richard as the Burfords turned their horses to leave, thanking Sir Richard for the loan of the horses and carts, comestibles and information.

They entered the town, which was now virtually deserted, only minutes after their arrival. As they passed the market square, there was the woman lying on the ground, moaning with no one near her. The three of them gave her a wide berth and turned north toward Northton. No one was leaving the town on the west road as this passed through Clanfield and entry to the town was being blocked. Whether or not anyone had come from Clanfield through Alvescot and Northton, they did not know.

Soon they were galloping through Northton and up the hill towards Swinbrook. On top of the hill they stopped at the Gloucester Road and looked back down the valley towards Beamtune. They could see the roads going north, south, east and west, but no one seemed to be going west. The road they were on was full of traffic, all going one way.

They continued down the hill and into Swinbrook where Lord Burford stopped at the inn on the bridge. As he entered the landlord touch his forelock and said, "My Lord, it is good to see you back."

"Thank you, and please send someone into the town to announce my return."

"I will do, sir."

Lord Burford left and remounted for the short ride to the back gate of Burford House which they found was already guarded to protect the house and those within from any refugee seeking sanctuary from the plague. One of the men at the gates said, "You are well come, sir, we all await your instructions as to how to face the threat."

When they entered the yard, the back door burst opened as the cook and kitchen staff flooded out to the arrival of their lord. Some fell to their knees and gave thanks to the Lord Christ for his return. As Lord Burford entered, along with Henry and Stephen, his wife, Mary, entered the kitchen along with his three daughters, Anne, Marion and Joan. Much expression of love and relief were shown. Now that the lord had returned, all would be well.

7

Back Home

There was no real bump this time as I landed almost perfectly on the settee back in my home. Immediately I looked at the clock on the DVD. It read 10:57 am. I looked at my watch and it said the same. I had been away for 2 hours and 17 minutes. This seemed a reasonable length of time to have walked to Brize Norton, have a chat with the priest and hurried back again. I had discovered that the passage of time in the other place was the same as the passage of time here.

Once more there was a moment that I wondered whether this has really happened, but really I had little doubt that it had. Yes, I had been to a different time. Not a different place, that was clear, but the same place in a different time. The only real question was how this had happened. Even this was a rather pointless question, as I doubted if I would ever know the answer and was sure that if I took my laptop to a computer expert and explained what had happened, he would be more likely to disbelieve me than to explain anything. Not only was it confusing as to why this had happened, but why it always takes me to the same place? Why the middle ages? Why at the beginning of the great plague? Was there any reason for this or was it sheer chance? I did not know and could not decide whether it was a good or a bad thing. Was it a great adventure for a young man or was it a dangerous game to play? Would I ever go back there again? I could not decide now, so I would simply listen to some cricket and get on with my day.

It was day two of the test and although it was a lovely sunny day in Carterton, it soon became clear that overnight rain in London had delayed the start of play at Lords. What to do now? Get something to eat? Beans on toast? Why not? It's quick, easy and tasty! It did not take long to prepare and ten minutes later I was sitting at the kitchen table eating. Having done so, my thoughts turned to Serene.

I dialled her land line as I knew her mobile was not working and waited for the ringing tone. Her sister answered and I asked to speak to Serene. She came on the line and I was pleased to hear some excitement in her voice. After the social niceties I asked, "What are you doing this afternoon?"

"Well, nothing I can't change."

"So would you like to go punting on the Cherwell?"

"Oh yes, you're a member of the school's boat team, aren't you?"

"Yes, but this is punting – no oars."

"Oh well, it's all the same to me. Can you pick me up?"

"Yes, I'll be there at 12:30 pm."

"That sounds good."

"Bye, then."

"Bye."

At the agreed time, I arrived at Serene's house and she came out to meet me. I was pleased to see she must have been waiting and I knew it must have been partly to avoid me meeting her family again. There's nothing wrong with her family, but I really didn't want to engage in niceties. She looked gorgeous in a tight blue top, red shorts and Jesus sandals. Soon we were speeding along the A40 towards

Oxford and I switched on the radio to see if play had started at Lords.

"Oh, I had forgotten you were big on cricket. Will we have to listen to it all afternoon?"

"I probably will, but I have an ear radio for when we are in the boat but it doesn't work in the car."

"I don't mind cricket, but couldn't listen to it all day."

Play had started and it was now 225 for 4.

We arrived at the Cherwell boathouse at 1:15 pm and, having paid to hire a boat, we were in it and pushed off before 1:30 pm I had paid for a three hour hire, so we had plenty of time as I pushed off upstream. Serene had never been in a punt or a boat before, but she clearly liked the experience as we punted upstream in the glorious sunlight. Soon she wanted to have a go at punting so I handed her the pole with a few simple instructions as to how to do it. As expected, she had no idea of what to do and hardly reached the river bed with the pole. The punt moved two feet forward at a time and she got little leverage. After a while, she got the hang of pushing but she had no ability to steer the thing. Soon the inevitable happened: we crashed into the river bank under an overhanging tree. This was no real problem and a bit of fun, so I got us back on track and told Serene to have another go. Despite the difficulties she was not put off at all and took the pole once more for another go. She was just getting the knack of it when she pushed the pole into the soft river bed and couldn't get it out again. The pole stayed where it was as the punt moved on, leaving us up a creak without a pole. We put our hands and arms in the water to slow our progress and then had to hand paddle back to get the pole. Eventually we did and pulled it out of the mud to continue our progress upstream.

It was my turn to punt for a while and on we went as Serene happily chatted and observed, "We should have brought a picnic basket."

"Yes, we should have, but we had no time to prepare anything. Next time we shall have to plan things."

"Oh, there's going to be a next time, is there?"

I was a little embarrassed but hoped she was joking about her inabilities to punt. It seemed she was and soon wanted to have another go.

"Okay, but if the pole gets stuck in the water again, don't let go of it."

She was getting better and although we were going from side to side, we where making progress, avoiding other boats and not hitting the bank.

"It's stuck again!"

"Don't let go! Pull it. Hold on."

This she did, but it resulted in the amazing sight of seeing Serene still holding onto the pole while the gap between the punt and the pole – with Serene clinging to it– widened. The pole was stuck at an angle and her weight slowly made the heavy top end of the pole bend towards the river. As if in slow motion, Serene inched closer and closer to the water, and she eventually gave up the struggle against the law of gravity when her bum touched the water and she let go. I stood and laughed heartily but then stopped as I thought she may be offended at my laughing at her plight. There was no need to worry because when she surfaced, she screamed, "Augggh, it's cold in here!" If that was her greatest concern, there was no real problem.

I didn't know if I should wait for her to swim over or to do the big male thing and dive in. It wasn't really my style, but soon I found myself in the water alongside Serene just because it all seemed part of the fun. We swam towards the punt but, of course, couldn't get in without tipping it over, so we pushed it against the bank before we climbed in. By now a couple of other punts were coming towards us to help and I called out to them that there was no problem, but one retrieved the pole and passed it over as they passed our punt. Both of us were dripping water all over the punt and I was glad I had decided to leave my ear radio in the car just in case I fell in. We laughed and fell into each other's arms. I remembered that part of the reason I liked Serene was because she was always up for a laugh and full of adventure. It was still very sunny and hot, so once we were out of the water we soon warmed up.

By now we were more than two hours into our three hour hire, so I took the pole and punted us downstream. It was a lot easier going back, not just because I was doing it, but because we were going with the flow of the river. Anyway, it's always quicker going back. Half an hour later we rounded the bend to see the boathouse and five minutes later the boatman held out his hand and I threw him the rope which he grabbed and tied around a post. He could see we had both been in the river and seemed to think this a little entertaining, but he didn't seem to mind that we had made the boat wet. After all, what would be expected if you let members of the public use your punt!

Soon we were in the mini and heading back to Carterton. Without thinking I drove straight to my house and then realised I was being a little presumptuous, but Serene didn't seem to mind as we walked in through the unlocked back door. Together we prepared some food. She fried some eggs and sausages as I made my own concoction of instant mashed potato, baked beans, and a large lump of yellow spread seasoned with salt and pepper. Sitting at the table Serene complimented me on my concoction and I praised her for not breaking the egg yolks.

Not long thereafter we were sitting on the settee with my laptop on a little stool next to it. I looked at it and thought about how I could raise the subject, but the kisses and cuddles soon started so I couldn't be bothered. About an hour later it was time to take Serene home as her parents had not seen her since they left for work in the morning and it was now after 7 pm. We pulled up outside her house and she took off her seat belt saying, "No kisses, as it's daylight and they know nothing other than that we are friends."

I understood and said, "Okay, when will I see you again?"

"Well, we have family coming around this weekend so it will have to be next week. Call me on Monday."

"Okay, bye." Next week seemed so far away, but I understood she had a life to live too and didn't have the 'luxury' of her family being away for ten weeks.

As she got out, I summoned up my courage and said, "When I do see you, I have something very important to tell you, so can you remind me if I forget to tell you?" "Okay." She smiled and closed the door. I hadn't told her but at least I had put myself in the position of *having* to tell her when we next met.

8

Preparations

Henry awoke to the sound of a kerfuffle in the courtyard below his window. Jumping out of bed and looking out he could see Scabbard organising other members of the household and people from the town. He had returned during the night with the luggage from London and Windsor and was already helping to prepare the town for its defence against the plague.

Henry dressed quickly and hurried down to find the house a buzz of activity. Word of his rising had already reached the kitchen and soon breakfast arrived as Henry's three sisters ran around fussing after their brother. They had not seen him for many weeks before his return last night when he had joined his father's party as it passed through Oxford on its way to Windsor. Henry had spent the last two years studying at Bulliol College and was now home for the summer. They had intended to spend a week in the royal household but news of the plague's progress had forced a change in plan.

During the meal, Lady Burford appeared and hugged her son. She had been busy organising the kitchen household whilst Lord Burford had given his orders to Scabbard who was now outside ensuring the town knew what was required. He was now elsewhere in the house writing letters to be sent to the surrounding farms and villages. Henry's father had been up for a long time and it seemed the only one not up and working was his brother, Stephen.

Having eaten, Henry sought his father.

"Ah, good morning, son. Did you sleep well?"

"Yes, Father, I am well refreshed and ready to play my part."

"Good, your learning at Oxford will do us well in the times ahead. I am nearly finished here, then we can both go to the town to ensure all is in place."

"Yes, Father, I shall order some horses to be prepared."

"Thank you, Henry. I will be with you soon."

As the sun approached its zenith, father and son were trotting out of the courtyard and through the gate to find about 10 or 12 people from outside the town trying to get into the town but being blocked by Lord Burford's men. The lord had given orders that no one was to be allowed in, except under exceptional circumstances and with the lord's expressed permission. However, many had brought supplies of food, clothing, firewood and, especially, vinegar that were being bought on Lord Burford's orders. The owners of these goods were sent back to their villages and farms to do their best to survive the pestilence. That morning, Lord Burford had given permission for only two people to be allowed in. They were two women both of whom had nursing and midwifery experience. Their skills may be useful in helping the nuns with the sick in the times to come.

As the two travelled the short distance down the hill to the bridge, the throng parted and hands were extended to their lord. The guards on the north bank of the Windrush river turned their pike as the two Burfords crossed the bridge into the town of Burford. As their lord passed, the people touched their forelocks in deference. Even though this was a requirement of the lower orders, there was still genuine affection for their lord. After all, he could be much worse. Henry was to inherit his father's title and it was somewhat fortuitous that as he reached the age of maturity, he was able to help his father, and the town, in this hour of need.

As they entered the town, Lord Burford could see the carcases of dead dogs and cats being cast into the river upstream and he called to a man. "You, my man, remind those people I gave orders for the animal carcases to be taken to the top of the hill and burnt outside the town." The two Burfords had discussed the arrangements to prepare for the plague and young Henry's learning about medical philosophy had advised that dead animals should be burnt. The lord turned to his son and said, "Yes, I know you said the bodies of the dead should be burnt too, but these good people have done nothing wrong. Should their lives be cut short, it would add to their suffering, and that of their families, if they were to be prevented from entering the kingdom of Heaven because their bodies had been burnt. That is a punishment reserved for traitors and heretics."

On the left was the town church of St. John the Baptist, part of the diocese of Gloucester. A little further on, and set back from the high street, was the abbey attached to the church. The nuns would be busy during the next few weeks and supplies were pouring in to assist in God's work. The street was full of traders and there was a buzz of activity, but no sense of summer excitement. Everybody was preparing for what would amount to a siege.

As father and son moved slowly through the throng, their presence was acknowledge by the people of the manor. "Good day, My Lord."

"Good day, Robin. I trust you and your family are well?"

"Yes, My Lord, they are all well and my wife, Rebecca, is helping in the abbey."

"Ah, I thought she would be. She is a good woman, your wife." Lord Burford squeezed his knees and his horse moved forward further up the hill followed by Henry.

Half way up they turned right into Sheep Street and immediately were met by a man running towards them. "My Lord, My Lord!"

"Yes, John, what is all the excitement?"

"I was coming to find you, sir. There are two men at the barrier wanting to come into the town. They are both from Northleach and say if they were allowed in, they could be of value to you and the town of Burford. One is the church priest and one is a barber surgeon."

"Oh yes, I have heard of the barber surgeon of Northleach." The lord paused for a while as he thought. "We have no barber surgeon in Burford and he would be of more use here than in a small town such as Northleach. I will allow him in, but, as for the priest, we have plenty of God's servants here and the people of Northleach will need their own priest. Tell him he... No, I will tell him myself."

The Burfords walked their horses along Sheep Street to where the road was blocked and supplies were being purchased from all sorts of traders. Lord Burford had made arrangements for the purchase of items deemed vital for the coming siege and his chancellor was overseeing the purchase, distribution and storage. As the Burfords approached the road block, the chancellor was dealing with a purchase and did not see the approaching lord and his son. "Sir John, how goes the day?"

Sir John rose from his seat at the table and spun around to greet his lord, having not seen him since before Lord Burford went off to get his sons from Oxford and London.

"Good day, My Lord. The day goes well and we have boosted the town's stores. But there are two men who have requested of you to be allowed into the town."

"Yes, I have heard," Lord Burford said and looked at the crowd where a priest stood out amongst the general peasants. Next to the priest was a well-dressed man whom Lord Burford assumed was the barber surgeon. He looked at the two men surrounded by peasants, all of whom were hoping they would be allowed into the town where they hoped they would be better able to survive the coming plague. They could not all possibly come in and it must be seen by all the people, especially those who are sent back to their own towns and villages, that those who are allowed in, are allowed in for very good reasons and not because of who they were.

Lord Burford beckoned to the priest and he approached obsequiously. "Father, I hear you wish to come and minister to the people of Burford?"

"Yes, My Lord, I can give the people comfort and pray for them."

"That is a very kind offer, but we have many of God's servants here and the people of Northleach need you more than we do." The priest opened his mouth to further plead his case but knew by the fact that Lord Burford's eyes have moved on that it was not open to negotiation. Lord Burford's eyes were now on the man he assumed was the barber surgeon. "You, sir. You are a barber surgeon?"

"Yes, sir, I am and with many years of practice."

"You can cut out buboes?"

"Yes, sir, and I have brought my knives." He held up a medium-size case he had in one hand. In his other hand was a larger case, presumably with his luggage in.

"You have come prepared. Go to the abbess and tell her I have sent you." The guards parted to allow him in whilst the priest stood looking forlorn.

"Sir John, do you know were Scabbard is?"

"I believe he is at the barrier on the Gloucester Road, sir."

The lord and Henry turned their horses and moved back along Sheep Street. Lord Burford moved closer to his son and whispered, "The priest is not needed here and word will go around the county that no one gets into Burford without a vital skill for the town. It will help maintain law and order to see fairness enacted in Burford. There may be riots of desperation ahead and turning away the priest will ensure no one can claim preference is given to anyone."

At the end of Sheep Street there was a caravan of hay wains moving down the road to be stored in the lord's barns. Once it had passed, father and son trotted up the hill towards the junction with Gloucester Road. They could see the smoke rising from the pyre on top of the hill and to the east. As planned, the smoke was blowing away from the town across the Windrush valley. Scabbard heard the horses and stood in the road as the Burfords approached. There was much noise on the other side of the barrier as Lord Burford said, "Good day, Scabbard. What is happening here?"

"Good day, sir. The people are objecting to being turned away and a man, his wife and 7 children are saying they have no home and nothing to eat."

Lord Burford looked at the family and asked in a loud voice, "What has happened to your home?"

"Our home is on the farm at Sherbourne and the landowner has said there will be no planting this winter, so there is no need for me and my family." Lord Burford showed no emotion and looked at the rest of the crowd. "You must all go back to your villages and your homes. There is no room for you here and you will be no worse off in your own homes and villages. Anybody who remains here in five minutes time will be arrested. Go back to your homes!"

He then turned his horse to indicate the matter was settled as the crowd mumbled their displeasure.

"Scabbard," called Lord Burford. "Give the family some food and some money and send them back to Sherbourne with a letter from me to the farmer telling him I will pay their rent over winter."

Back down the hill and at the corner of Witney Road they paused and surveyed the activities around them. Little was happening at the junction of the roads, so they trotted their horses to the end of the road where there was another barrier blocking those wishing to enter from there. All was quiet here with few wanting access to the town. Witney is to the east and away from the progress of the pestilence, so few people were likely to want to move towards the problem. Having praised the guards for their vigilance, the lord and his son trotted back along Witney Road and back into the High Street.

Slowly they rode down the hill to the bridge where the crowd on the other side had grown. Once more the lord addressed the people telling them they must return to their villages and homes as there was no room for them in Burford and they would be no less safe in their own homes. Any one remaining after five minutes would be arrested. The Burfords crossed the bridge and the crowd parted in weary resignation. Then they went up the hill and into Burford house once more where Anne, Marion, Joan and Stephen greeted their father and brother.

That night the whole household – family and servants – prepared to go to the church of St. John the Baptist to ask the Lord for deliverance from the pestilence. In the beautiful evening sunlight the household made their way out of the courtyard towards Burford, all on foot in order of social importance. At the front was the Burford family and behind came the household with the men in the front, the senior female house staff and the Angles, Saxons and Welsh in the rear.

Down the hill and over the bridge went the Burford party and as they approached St. John the Baptist's, the whole of Burford was waiting for them to enter first. The crowd parted to allow passage and the Burfords took up their rightful place at the front of the church. Others took their seats in their social order with the Welsh at the very back. There were only two of them apart from one Welsh servant girl who was part of the Burford household..

The priest began by welcoming the Burfords back to the town and thanking God for their return. He then went through the mass as if the congregation were not there. Having completed the ritual, the priest asked for God to save the town and its pious people from the sickness and commanded the people to increase their prayers to the one true God.

Once the ritual was over, the Burfords left the church whilst all others waited for them to pass. Once outside they made their way towards the bridge, but as Lord Burford and Lady Mary got onto the bridge, there was a commotion behind them. A man was pushing through the throng towards the Burfords, shouting, "Lord Burford, Lord Burford!"

Lord Burford stopped and shouted, "Allow him through!"

The man pushed his way to the bridge and immediately blurted out, "One of the nuns is ill and showing every sign of the sickness."

9

Mundane Life

The next few days passed slowly and I filled my time with usual summer things such as sunbathing in the garden and listening to the end of the test match. This had been a tight match with Australia needing 367 in the last innings but only 81 overs to do it in. England failed to get all 10 wickets and Australia failed to get the 367 runs. So, a draw. Now all I needed to restore normality was a couple of nights out with my friends, but first a phone call to Serene to arrange a night out with her early in the new week.

The phone began to ring at the other end and I hoped Serene would answer.

"Hello, Edmund. How are you?"

"I'm fine, Serene, how did your weekend go?"

"Oh, you know, just family stuff. What have you been doing?"

"Not a lot really. My days are a bit boring to be honest. So, when are you free, Serene?"

"Okay, well not tonight, but how about tomorrow night?"

"All right, I'd like to go to the cinema if you don't mind?"

"Well, what do you want to see?"

"There's an old Harry Potter film on I missed the first time around if you haven't seen it?"

"Well, I will be honest, Edmund, and tell you that I'm sure I've seen that one but I'm more than happy to see any Harry Potter film again."

"All right, it starts early, at 7:15 pm, so let's go there first and then move on to Triumph's for a few drinks and to see the crowd."

"Yes, that's good. Can you pick me up at about 6:30 pm?"

"Sure, see you at 6:30 pm then. Bye, Serene."

"Bye, Edmund."

I was missing my family and when Serene was away for the weekend, I did think about her a lot. Now that she was back and we had made a date, I was really looking forward to seeing her again. That night was passed watching television and thinking how I was going to handle the subject with Serene as I had told her to remind me if I did not mention it. How could I possibly tell her the full story? Should I just let it drop? I couldn't really do that as I had already raised the subject of *something* with Serene, but I could talk about something less unbelievable. Anyway, we shall see what happens.

The next day, I cut the grass as I had promise my parents I would do. It gave me a bit of exercise, helped me top up my suntan and filled a few hours. When I had finished, I was hot and sweaty so it was into the shower to get ready for Serene. At 6:30 pm I was outside Serene's house waiting for her to come out. I sat and waited but no Serene. Was she playing games or just being a woman? I'm not sure, but after 5 or 6 minutes she appeared and apologised for keeping me waiting. What had seemed vitally important 10 seconds earlier didn't seem important at all now. I gave her a kiss and off we sped.

A quarter of an hour later we were parked at the cinema and walking towards the desk. To my surprise, Serene said, "This one's on me."

I didn't argue as she offered her money to the cashier and I said, "Thank you." We walked into the cinema and settled down. It was almost empty, probably because everyone else had seen the film a long time ago. We could have had a good kiss, cuddle and fondle, but really wanted to watch the film. When it was finished, I was glad I had seen it as it seemed to complete my Harry Potter education. I said to Serene, "You must have been bored."

"No, not at all. Just because I had seen it before didn't make any difference. I still enjoyed it. After all, I had read the book before I saw it the first time, so I knew what was going to happen. You had read the book before too, so did you enjoy it?"

"Yes, I did, and thank you again for taking me. Let's get off to Triumph's."

There had been no mention of what I had wanted to talk to her about and I couldn't decide if that was pleasing or displeasing. It meant I did not have to explain the inexplicable and, for some reason I could not explain to myself, I felt the need to tell her about what had happened. Why I just didn't know, as I was not even sure it had happened myself and I had decided never to try it again. Or would I? As the time since I last travelled – as I have come to think of it – passes, I find myself feeling less appreciative of a lucky escape and more curious about what else is out there. I know it's a silly thing to even think about, but what's the point of being an indestructible youth if I don't take risks?

In Triumph's we met up with a few friends, one of whom had an older sister which made it easier to get a drink. Not that that was any use to me as I had to drive home. I was beginning to realise there was a downside to being able to drive. I see now why groups have *one* designated driver and take it in turns, as it's not a lot of fun being the only sober one. It's also pretty boring having to deal with those who have drunk quite a lot and are getting very verbose, talking nonsense thinking it's all very profound, intuitive and insightful.

Jade walked in and this was the first time I had seen her since I tried my luck at my birthday party. I looked at her and she did look very tasty, but since then things had developed with me and Serene. Would she remember I tried to chat her up and would it make any difference to our long term school friendship now that I was with Serene? Did she even know Serene and I were an item? Were Serene and I an item?

Jade walked up to me and with no sense of embarrassment said, "Hello, Edmund."

I was relieved and replied, "Hello, Jade."

"Hello, everybody!" she shouted above the music and chatter. "This is my friend, Eva. Eva's Polish, so if any of you need any cleaning doing whilst she's in town, just shout!" This was followed by a mixture of raucous laughter and embarrassed silence. Eva just stood there looking blank.

As the night passed, I wandered around and found myself talking to a group of men who were dressed, not very convincingly, in woman's clothing. As we were chatting I remarked, "I assume you are all off to a fancy dress party?"

They all fell about laughing and one said, "No, we were all meant to be going to Afghanistan today, but our flight has been delayed. However, all our kits and clothes are on the aeroplane, so we had to borrow clothes from any woman we could find on the base."

"Oh well, at least you are not wasting your time sitting on the base doing nothing," I responded. "So, you're all RAF blokes then?"

"No, none of us are RAF. We're all Royal Marines. We're just here to fly out. We've never been to Brize Norton before and we were told Witney's where it all happens around here."

"I suppose it is as the only other places around here are all villages."

"Yeah, most of you talk like country bumpkins"

"Do we?"

"Yeah, lots of unnecessary 'Os' are thrown into words. It sounds like 'Oi loike to go for a roide oin moi boike'." He and his friends thought this very funny and I wandered off.

It was getting late and I knew Serene couldn't be home too late, but I was hoping to take her back to my place before I had to get her home. However, she was having fun and drinking and although she was not as drunk as some others, she showed no sign of wanting to leave. Was she just having fun with our mutual friends or was she getting over me? I had no idea and had I been alone, I would have left but, of course, I had to take Serene home. Time was now dragging and I made a note to myself not to go out with people drinking if I cannot. How much longer and would it mean I wouldn't be able to take Serene back to my place first?

I wondered around chatting to anybody and noticed there was something happening outside. It seemed the Marines were involved in a fracas. I pushed my way outside along with most of the club. It seems a few locals had tried to pick a fight with the Marines. Whether this was because they were all dressed in women's clothing or because they were big blokes who looked capable of looking after themselves, was not clear. Maybe it was a bit of both. Anyway, the bouncers had broken things up and now a couple of police officers arrived. After a while, the police left with all the Marines. I don't think they were arresting them, but just escorting them to a taxi to take them back to

Brize Norton. I wouldn't have minded that myself, as the officers who were 'taking the situation in hand' were a couple of fit women.

By now it was nearly chucking out time and people were starting to drift away. As Serene and I were leaving, the inevitable happened and I was assailed by a chorus of, "Give us a lift, Edmund!" What could I say? Three people in the back seat of a mini is quite a squeeze, but Serene could sit next to me. The bad news was that they all got dropped off in order and that meant Serene was dropped off before the last one and I was left to go home alone. Rather depressed I got home and went straight to bed thinking there must be a better way to spend the summer. And what might that be?

I awoke the next morning feeling the same way and mulling over once more whether I should 'travel' again? The reasons for doing so – excitement, education, fate – seemed to be heavier than the reasons against it, which was the mere problem of never returning. As I was cogitating the pros and cons, my mobile rang.

"Hello?"

"Hello, Edmund, how are you?"

"Oh, I'm fine, Serene. How about you?"

"Well, I do have to admit I have a bit of a hangover".

"Ha ha! *I* haven't got one."

"No, you wouldn't, would you, Edmund?"

"No."

"But, that's why I'm calling, really. To say sorry for last night."

"Why?"

"Well, I did get a little drunk and I think I ignored you after we had seen Harry Potter."

"Oh, that's all right. I was happy to see you enjoying yourself." *What a liar I am!* "Anyway, Edmund, you said you needed to tell me something and I was to remind you."

Oh, my God! This was crunch time. What was I to say? I had virtually decided to travel again and thought I needed to tell at least someone if I never returned. Perhaps telling her on the phone would be easier than face to face. "I, er, well, I was on my laptop the other day and as I typed in the URL 'bbc.co.uk/cricket', I started to fly off to some other place in a cloud."

I heard a little laugh at the other end. I was aware of how silly this sounded and didn't mind making a joke of it as I was sure she would remember it if I did not return. "When the cloud cleared, I was in another place and didn't know what to do. Eventually I clicked 'undo' and found myself back at home."

"Riiight," said Serene.

"Then, later, I thought I'd try again and the same thing happened. This time when I got to the other place I started walking around and went towards a church in the distance. On the way I met a very smelly man who was tending to sheep. I tried talking to him but could hardly understand what he was saying. The church looked very like the one in Brize Norton. You know, St. Britius?"

"Yes, I know it."

"Well, the priest came out of the church and invited me in. We chatted and I realised I was in St. Britius, but it was the middle of the 14th century and the Black Death was about to arrive."

"Yes, Edmund, do you think you may have been watching too much Harry Potter?" "Okay, maybe, but I am going back and maybe for some time, so if you don't see me for a while, you will know why."

"Okay, Edmund, give me a call when you get back from 'the other place'," she said with exaggerated sincerity.

"Will do. Bye, Serene."

"Bye, Edmund."

I knew she would not believe me, but at least if I didn't get back she would have some idea of why and would think I was just dumping her. Her call had also made me feel good for knowing that she hadn't lost interest in me. I now felt a new confidence that I could go travelling again without everybody thinking I had just disappeared.

I spent the rest of the day preparing what to take, thinking of what I might need and making sure it was as little stuff from the 21st century as possible. I'd take a brown backpack made of artificial fibres which I could say was cotton. I knew the middle of the 14th century was a strong, rich wool society but I think they knew of Indian cotton. My clothes would all be something that looked like wool or cotton, but I'd avoid bright colours which they probably didn't have then. Should I or should I not wear a watch? As mine is an analogue watch, I decided I could get away with it. I think the Swiss were making mechanical clocks at the time so I could say it was just a little one. However, I finally decided this would be an unnecessary problem should the question of 'what is that' ever come up so I would leave it behind. After all, everybody in the 14th century survived without one, so I could.

The biggest problem would be why I didn't have any transport, like a horse? I'd have to say I had a horse but it had run off when it was frightened. As for my funny English, I could say I came from a land to the east and my English was not too good. I could keep my real name, as Edmund was a name used at the time I believe. It's just as well my parents didn't name me Wayne or Damion. Decovny would fit in too as I am told it is a name derived from my father's Russian ancestors. A thousand thoughts ran through my head and I was pretty sure I could come up with an answer if I had to. Serene had not believed me, but I hoped anyone in the 14th century would find me more convincing. I went to bed that night ready, ordinance wise and psychologically, for the next day.

As for food, I had been to the supermarket the day before and bought some German black bread as I was sure they did not have processed, white bread in the 14th century. I think that was a 20th century invention from Chorley Wood. I used this bread to make sandwiches and into them I wanted to put my favourite, peanut butter, but thought I'd better stick with jam as they would have had fruit and some sort of sweet preservative then. Along with the sandwiches I got some plums, apples and pears. There were some lovely bananas in the kitchen but I thought I'd better avoid them. Too exotic! As for liquid, I had got away with the plastic bottle last time when talking to the priest, so I put some apple cordial into it. If I shared it with someone, I could explain away the taste of apples. I could even tell them it was weak cider!

The next morning, I awoke when the alarm went off at 6 am It had already been light for at least two hours, so the sun was full in the eastern sky. I had a good breakfast of cereal and toast, rather than one or the other, and finished it off with the banana I though I'd better not take with me. Then I went to clean my teeth. As I looked in the mirror, I saw a new, confident teenager who was determined to take whatever chances life had to offer. I was ready for the next stage of the adventure.

Before I set off, I wondered if the weather was the same here as in the other place, just like the time and other things, so I opened the door and looked at the sky. There were a couple of clouds but not much else. I put my backpack on, which is not comfortable whilst sitting on the sofa, and put the laptop on my lap. The blue whirligig was sticking out of the backpack. Opening up the laptop, I logged on. I typed in the usual URL of 'bbc.co.uk/cricket'. As expected, the mist gathered and the room swirled. 20 seconds later the mist cleared and I could see myself in the field once more surrounded by sheep who didn't seem at all perturbed by my sudden arrival. At this, I wondered if I had just arrived or if I had merely moved into another time to take my place in a body that was just sitting there waiting. Who knows? I certainly didn't.

I looked around and there was nobody in sight, so I stood up and looked towards the bush I hid the laptop in last time. There it was, so I pulled the whirligig out of the backpack and stuck it in the place I had just got up from. Then I remembered I had looked at the sky before leaving, so I looked up at this sky. There were no distinguishable clouds, just a layer of overnight cumulus stratus. So, the weather was not the same in this place even if the time was. Putting the laptop inside its case and walking towards the bush to hide it, I reflected on how differently I felt this time as opposed to my last travel. Now I was confident and secure. I wasn't necessarily secure in my safe return but secure in that I knew what I was doing and that I would make things happen rather than let things just happen to me.

I now knew where I was in this other place and had a choice between two towns: Witney or Burford. Witney was 7 miles away and Burford was 5 miles away. A no brainer really, so, looking at the sun I headed north, as far as I could tell, towards Burford.

10

The Pestilence Arrives

Immediately, and without comment, the Burfords turned towards the abbey. Then Lord Burford stopped and said to his wife and younger children, "No, Henry and I shall go. You must not put yourselves at risk."

His wife, Anne, wanted to protest, but would never argue with her husband in the presence of the common people. As they made their way towards the abbey, much of the population of Burford hurriedly dispersed, thinking their homes would provide some security from the sickness, crossing themselves as they went.

The Burfords arrived at the door and the abbess greeted them. Young Henry had been studying apothecary and the medical philosophers at Oxford, and now was the time to put his knowledge into action. His studies had been an academic exercise with no intention whatsoever of becoming a physician by trade. Trade was not for one of the Burfords. However, it was important for the lord of the manor to show concern and take a lead in looking after the sick. The nuns and others needed to be set a good example and young Henry's knowledge would be invaluable. Irrespective of the need for a public show, the Burfords did have genuine concern for the people of the manor.

The Burfords approached the door and it was opened for them before they reached it. They entered, ignoring the fawning of the sister who opened the door, and simply asked, "Where is the sick sister?"

"This way, sir." The sister led the way through the abbey.

Henry strode into the nun's sickroom followed by his father. On the bed was a youngish woman in nun's habit, Sister Cecilia, making a continuous, low moaning noise. Henry knew her, as he did all of the nuns and most of the town, and as he approached her, he could see she was dripping with sweat and immediately diagnosed, "A yellow bile problem!"

He lifted her arm and could see buboes developing. Along with this tell tale sight was the confirming stench associated with the Black Death; the smell of rotting flesh. Henry put down her arm and walked towards the door to take a deep breath of fresh air.

At this point, the abbess arrived and curtsied deeply to the Burfords. Lord Burford nodded but young Henry did not look away from Sister Cecilia, saying, "This is a summer ailment and must be treated with purging and blood letting."

The abbess informed him, "She already has a bad case of diarrhoea, sir."

"Nevertheless, we must void the body of the imbalanced humour. Give her hellebore."

"Give her what, sir?"

"Hellebore, but if you have none, then salt water or mustard will suffice."

"How do you know this?" asked Lord Burford.

"This is the accepted regimen prescribed by the Islamic philosopher Avicenna."

Henry then turned to the abbess and advised, "If there is no improvement by the morning, open a vein. The humour must be allowed to leave the body and return it to balance."

"Yes, sir." The abbess nodded deferentially.

Lord Burford instructed the abbess to say special prayers for the nun, to which the abbess replied, "The sisters are already in the chapel asking our Lady for intercession in our sister's ailment."

"Take her clothing and all her belongings and burn them before dowsing the room in much vinegar," Henry advised further.

"Sir, other than her clothing, she has no belongings."

"No, but you must also burn anything you think she may have used in the last few days."

"Yes, sir."

"And put flowers all around the abbey to stave off the smell of the sickness and prevent it from being passed to the other nuns through the air."

"Certainly, sir."

The Burfords walked towards the door and into the fresh night air. Outside was a small gathering of people at some distance from the abbey and Lord Burford walked towards them saying, "Go to your homes. There is nothing to be done here and my son and heir, Henry, has expressed his medical opinion informed by years of study at Oxford. In the morning you must all gather flowers and put them about your homes so that you do not catch the sickness from the foul odours. There is nothing more to be done other than to pray for all our deliverance. We are all in the hands of the good Lord and our Lady."

With this the people slowly moved off and the two Burfords walked briskly towards the bridge, up the hill and into the manor house.

Once inside, the house cook was informed to serve dinner. The rest of the house had been waiting for the return of Lord Burford and Henry and soon the whole family was seated and tucking into their food. Over the meal, the talk was of nothing other than the sickness. Henry talked of the four humours and Avicenna, Hippocrates and Socrates. With all this knowledge the family, and the common people of Burford, were lucky to have the benefit of Henry's education.

"How had the sickness arrived?" asked Henry's mother.

"Maybe in some supplies brought in or contact with someone from outside the town," answered Henry.

"I doubt that anyone with the sickness would have entered the town," opined Lord Burford. "Even if they had, they would still be here and probably sick as well."

"Yes, but someone who came back in may have been with someone who had the sickness."

"But no one else is sick," added Stephen.

Not yet, but some people may show the sickness quicker than others, thought Henry, *and their sickness may not yet be showing, or they may be sick at home and their families are keeping quiet out of fear of being locked in with them.*

After the meal, all retired to bed quickly but there was a new sombre atmosphere in the house. The much feared sickness had arrived. No one was sure how it had arrived, but all the attempts to keep Burford separate from the rest of the world had failed. With Henry's help, the town may be able to fight the sickness, but no one was really sure what to do. Everybody would have to wait for the sickness to take its course. But how long that would take, no one knew.

Early the next morning, Henry was up and soon talking to his father about what was needed. Lord Burford called Scabbard to join the conference and the father and son instructed him on what was necessary, but first Lord Burford asked, "Scabbard, what's the news on Sister Cecelia?"

"Sir, the news is that she is no better but still alive."

"We thank the Lord Christ for sparing her through the night," observed the lord.

Henry then instructed Scabbard, "You must give instructions to gather flowers and put them about the house. All those that are not put about the house, must be made into posies for the family to carry at all times. Any loose petals must be crushed and made into a perfume to spread on clothes to ward off the miasma. The household will need these when going out and all those attending the sick must be told to do the same."

"Yes, sir, I shall ensure all is done this morning."

"We must also inform the outside world that the sickness has arrived in Burford," said Lord Burford. "Send two men in each group to go north, south, east and west to inform and to gather information on what is happening."

"Certainly, sir, I shall ensure all is done immediately."

Scabbard gave a shallow bow and turned to leave.

Once outside, Scabbard called men and passed on the instructions of the two Burfords. Edgar and Knut were instructed to ride to Alvescot, Clanfield, Bourton, Beamtune and Norton to inform and gather information of the disease's progress. Up the hill they rode towards the Gloucester Road. The entrance to the town was still guarded to prevent entry and Edgar informed the guards of Lord Burford's instructions and they were allowed out. The earlier attempts by those of the surrounding villages to gain entry to Burford seemed to have dissipated. Probably word had gone around the county that Burford would not provide a place of refuge for anyone except its permanent residents.

The barrier was opened for Edgar and Knut to pass and the two men rode briskly towards Alvescot. As they entered the hamlet, there was no sign of anyone, so the two stopped and dismounted. A voice emerged from the shadows asking, "What do you want?"

Edgar replied, "We have come from Lord Burford to ask if the village needs anything and to inform you that the sickness has reached Burford, but we two are not sick."

"Sick or not, stay away from us," came the gruff response.

"Are all well in the village?" asked Knut.

"I know of no sickness but all stay in their homes and some may be hiding the sickness to avoid being locked into their homes."

"Is there anything you need?" asked Knut.

"Nothing you can provide, thank you. Now only the good Lord Christ can help us."

With this, the two emissaries got back on their horses and headed towards Clanfield – the first settlement in Oxfordshire to be struck by the disease. As they approached the village, men of Clanfield saw them coming and began to wave the two riders away. The men reigned in their horses some distance from the village and Knut shouted, "We come with news from Burford on the instruction of the lord. It seems likely the sickness has come to Burford as one of the nuns is showing signs of the ailment."

One villager shouted back, "We are sorry to hear your news."

Knut then asked, "What of the sickness in Clanfield?"

"There are now three houses closed up and all the village is in much despair."

Edgar shouted, "Have you all you need in the village?"

"No, sir, we have not. Our food stocks will not last long and we ask you to inform Lord Burford of this so that he might help us."

Edgar replied, "When we return, Lord Burford will be informed and we are sure he will send what he can for the people of Clanfield."

"Thank you kind, sirs. Please tell the lord of our loyalty and fare you well."

The two men urged their horses towards Bourton and as they approached, they could see a barrier across the road but no guards. Were all the people dead? As they drew closer, men came running out waving staffs and pikes at the two riders. They stopped their horses and shouted they were from Lord Burford to gather information on the sickness and to inform them that it had reached Burford. One of the Bourton men shouted, "All of Bourton is sickness free and if you try to enter, we will have to kill you. We hope you, and Lord Burford, will understand."

"Yes, we do," Knut shouted back. "Our lord has asked us to ask you if there is anything the people of Bourton need."

After a silence the response came. "We could do with some ale as there is little to drink here and the stream is inadequate for our needs."

"We shall inform the lord and he may be able so send some barrels. We wish you well and hope the sickness never descends upon the good people of Bourton."

The two riders turned back to the Clanfield-Beamtune Road and onto Sir Richard's town. Edgar said, "Bourton is lucky that it is not on the road to Beamtune and so few people pass through the village."

"Yes, and I have heard the people of Bourton are very godly," added Knut.

As the two came close to Beamtune, once more they were met by waving guards who warned them to stay away. Knut shouted the same as before and the reply came that many had fallen sick in Beamtune, but that Sir Richard was content the town had all it needed in the short term and Lord Burford was to be thanked for his concern. Edgar shouted back, "May the Lord be with you all,"

Then he began to ride around the back of the church towards Northton. Apart from the church, there were few buildings in Northton so it was little surprise no one stopped them from entering the village.

It was silent as they approached and no one was to be seen. Edgar and Knut dismounted and tied their horses to a tree before walking through the graveyard towards the church door.

As they went to the door, Knut called, "Is anybody here?"

There was no response. They opened the door and walked in cautiously to find the church empty. No one was praying and the priest was nowhere to be found. Where were the few inhabitants of the village? Where was the priest? Had they all died? Had they all fled? Even the priest? There were no answers to be found here, so the two men remounted their horses and headed towards Alvescot once more.

They came to the cross of the Bourton and Burford roads and turned north to head home. Soon they saw a lone figure walking north and Knut said to Edgar, "We had better see who he is and where he is going?" As they approached the figure, he stopped and turned towards the approaching riders. He was a young man looking rather unusual and as if he did not belong here. "Who are you, sir?" called Knut from a safe distance.

"I am Edmund Decovny," came the reply.

"Edmund De Covny, do you have the sickness?"

"No, I do not."

"Where is your horse?"

"Something frightened her and she ran off."

"Then you had better get on the back of my horse and come with us to Lord Burford."

Immediately, Edmund realised that this was not really a request and did as he was bid, but found it very difficult to get on a horse without any stirrups. Knut helped him up and before he knew what was happening, they sped towards Burford.

11

Henry and Edmund

As we galloped across the field, I thought to myself that I had prepared an explanation for my lack of horse but never thought I would be using it so quickly. No sooner had I hidden my laptop under the bush than I found myself effectively a prisoner. Already I was regretting my foolhardy decision to travel again.

Soon our two horses and three men were going down into the Shilton dip and on our left, to the west, I could see a few hovels near the stream. Up in front was what would later become the A40. Straight ahead I could see   men gathered looking towards us, and the three of us were heading in their direction.

When we approached, Edgar was in front of Knut and I could just about hear Edgar speaking to the assembled men as he reined his horse in. "We have found a stranger by the name of Edmund de Covny whom we must take to Lord Burford. He says he is free of the sickness and looks in good health."

By now Knut and I were by Edgar's side as Edmund heard the man who seemed to be in charge say,

"All right, if you are sure you may bring him into the town, but *you* are answerable to Lord Burford, not *me*!"

The barrier was raised and the three of us passed through. I was aware that all eyes were on me as we passed and proceeded towards the town. There was no hotel on the corner at the top of the hill, but soon there were houses on either side of the road almost recognisable as those still standing in the 21st century. The three moved quite slowly as the streets were full of people; almost as many as on a summer's day in my own time. To my left, I could see a turning which I assumed would later become Sheep Street. Further down there was no pelican crossing and no supermarket, but the noise was becoming louder and louder. By now there were cobble stones underfoot and the noise of the horses' hooves echoed against the buildings on either side. This noise was added to by the noise of other horses' hooves, the wheels of carts on the cobbles and the shouts of people above this cacophony on what seemed to be market day. There were vendors on either side selling all kinds of goods, mainly comestibles, and the whole town stank of all sorts of unpleasant odours, the most prominent of which was horse manure. I looked down and could see it was everywhere, so much so that the horses were almost wading through it. It seemed that it had not occurred to anyone to clean it up! As a consequence, there were millions of flies around and by now many were beginning to feast on me. In front, and to my right, I could see the St. John the Baptist church, but from what I could remember of the church this one was a little smaller, as though bits were missing. Either it was not the same church or bits had been added on after the time I was in now.

Once again I became aware that people were looking at me and I didn't know if this was because I was a stranger to the town or because I looked strange. Either way, I was on my way to see Lord Burford, whoever that was, and this seemed as though it would determine my future. Merely 10 minutes ago I was a free man in Carterton of the 21st

century and now I was effectively a prisoner in the 14th century. What was I to do? There was nothing I could do except rehearse his story about how I came to be wondering in the Cotswolds and create my new background. Anything I told my captors would sound more convincing than the truth.

The three of us proceeded towards the bridge over the Windrush river, but instead of the beautiful 'old' stone bridge, there was a wooden structure that amounted to little more than a few planks laid on a couple of stone pillars on either side of the river with the water lapping around the stone pillars. As the horses mounted the bridge, I had the chance to experience a new way of crossing a river I had crossed many times before. This crossing was much slower and I had the opportunity to look up and down stream as we passed. But where were we going? By the 21st century there was nothing on the other side of the bridge, so where were they going in the 14th century? As I was used to, the road forked on the other side of the river and there was a choice of going towards Chipping Norton or towards Stowe. The two horses took the right fork towards Chippy and, set back from the road, was a large house with a driveway coming down towards what would later be the A361. A few moments passed and the horses turned right into the driveway of the large house.

Was this where Lord Burford lived? Was this an ancient building long since demolished so that there was no trace of it in the 21st century? Was this all still a dream? Then a new thought entered my head: Was it because the computer induced some sort of hypnotic state that made me think this was all real? The idea of closing my eyes and screaming, '*This is not happening*' occurred to me, but I thought better of it. Whether or not this was all real, he would have to deal with it as if it were real. It reminded me of the philosophy lesson at school where the whole class had sat around discussing whether or not the table they were at would still exist if it were not perceived be anyone. The class had concluded that even if it did not exist, they had better behave as if it did, for the consequences could be pretty painful if they had walked into it convinced it was not really there.

As Edgar and Knut walked the horses down the driveway, with me still on the horse, a man came towards us.

"Knut, who is this you have with you?" asked the man.

"He calls himself Edmund de Covny, Scabbard, and he says he does not have the sickness." *Scabbard*, I thought to myself. *I must remember that!* "He certainly looks well and he says he lost his horse when she was frightened, so we thought Lord Burford would want to help a Norman wondering in the fields".

"You have done well, Knut and Edgar. Lord Burford would want this man to be brought to him."

Suddenly I realised that it was not just my 'old fashioned' first name that fitted in well in the 14th century but that my surname was being misinterpreted as **D e Covny** and not Decovny as it should be spelled. My name isn't French or Norman. In fact, as far as I can remember, my family name had Russian-Jewish origins. My mind raced back to my history lessons. Weren't the Jews driven out of England less than a hundred years before the time I was in now, accused of bringing disease, the evidence for which was that the Jews didn't get diseases nearly so much? *Of course*! It's perfectly logical. It couldn't have anything to do with the kosher dietary requirements which meant their lives were so much cleaner than the rest of the people. *Yes, 1290*, I thought, *and that was under Edward I.* My research to prepare for this travel had informed me that the 'present' king was Edward III, so Edward I must have been his grandfather. It's probably best to play along with the Norman ancestry assumption, rather than to tell them I had Jewish ancestry. Anyway, my father never felt Jewish anymore than my mother felt Christian. I didn't suppose telling my new captors that being Jewish was through the mother's line because, as Jewish women are not sexual beings, they couldn't possibly get pregnant with anybody other than their Jewish husbands. There were no genetic tests in those days. Yes, it's best to play along with being Norman. But how to behave in the presences of my 'betters'? The only thing to do was to follow the cues from others.

Knut half turned and looked at me, which I took to be an instruction to dismount. Although I can just about ride, I am certainly not a horseman and holding on with my legs had left my thigh muscles a little aching. Scabbard had already disappeared into Burford house and as I was stretching my aching muscles, a man appeared at the door and Edgar and Knut suddenly acquired slightly weak knees and a stooped posture.

"Sir, this is Edmund de Covny," said Knut.

"I have heard, Edgar. Thank you both."

As Lord Burford turned to me a young man arrived at his side. "Come along in, de Covny. I am Lord Burford and this is my son, Henry."

No hand was offered, so Edmund did not offer his. Lord Burford and Henry stepped aside as I entered.

"I hear you have lost your horse, de Covny."

"Yes, she ran off when something frightened her and I was unable to catch her again."

"When was this?"

"Oh, er, not long before Edgar and Knut found me."

"I will send Edgar and Knut out again to look for her. Henry, take Edmund to the kitchen and get him some food."

"Certainly, Father."

Oh dear! Now they are going to look for a horse that won't be there. What a tangled web we weave when first we practice to deceive.

"Follow me please, Edmund," Henry said as he walked through to another part of the house.

He called me Edmund, so I assume I can call him Henry. As the son of the lord, he must be the heir to the title and the estate of Lord Burford, I assume.

I followed Henry through to the kitchen where Henry asked the genuflecting cook to prepare a meal for me. Henry then walked through to another room, where I followed, and Henry indicated that I should sit down.

"So, tell me how you came to be wandering, horseless outside the town?"

"As you know, my horse was frightened away."

"What I meant was how you came to be there at all. Where are you from and what was the purpose of your journey?"

I had prepared for this and now was the time to relay the story I had created. Certain parts would have to be spontaneous as I now knew I was meant to be Norman.

"My family currently live in Saxony where I grew up and I was on my first travel to England. It has taken me many weeks to get here and then I lost my horse."

"Oh, I see, that goes to explain your strange accent. You speak French?"

Oh God! He would expect me to speak French if I was an educated Norman. What now? I do speak French but it's modern French. I summoned up a few words in French telling him I also spoke French with a strange accent. Henry seemed to understand, so I assumed French had developed less in the last 700 years than English had. I quickly reverted to my best Chaucerian English and hoped I had got away with it.

Changing the subject, I said, "But tell me about you and your life."

"As you can see, I live here and I am studying at Balliol College, Oxford. It was founded in 1263 by John de Balliol the wealthy Scottish Lord."

"Oh yes, what are you studying?" I enquired

"Greek, Latin and medicine."

"Medicine! So you know a bit about the current epidemic?"

"The what? E-pi-de-mic! That's a good word for it. It arises suddenly and is everywhere. You mean the sickness?"

"Yes, the sickness. Tell me what you are doing to fight it." I asked hoping to keep the subject off me.

A teenage girl appeared with a large plate on a tray and put it in front of me. "Thank you, Megan," said Henry.

"Yes, thank you Megan. It's very kind of you," I added whilst looking at the girl whom I thought would be very attractive if she had washed her hair and had some decent clothes. This was clearly difficult in the 14th century, especially if she is poor.

Megan curtsied and gave me a flirtatious look as she left the room.

"A pretty girl."

"Yes, she is Welsh, of course, but she is of no danger. Her family were all killed in an uprising," Henry mentioned casually.

"So, how did she get here?"

"She was brought back by a Burford man in the king's army and my father gave her work in the house. This was about 5 years ago."

By now, I was staring at my plate as I had never seen so much meat in my life. It had not been long since I had breakfast, but I knew I had to eat as much as possible as I was supposed to have been found wandering. My backpack, with some food in it, had been taken from me as I dismounted and I had no idea where it was now.

"So, as you were saying, about the sickness?" I asked.

"We have ordered the killing of all the cats and dogs as a start..."

I lost all restraint and blurted out, "Oh no, that's the worst thing you can do!"

Henry looked bemused and said, "But they spread the sickness."

"No. they don't. The fleas on the black rat spread the sickness."

"Eh, rats?" Enquired Henry somewhat surprised.

"Yes, rats. That's why you must not kill the cats and dogs because they kill the rats."

Henry looked very confused. "What makes you think that?"

I had given some thought to this question as part of my preparations to travel. "Where I come from, the sickness, or the Black Death as we call it, has already passed through and we have learnt many things. There are three sorts of this plague and you have what is known as bubonic plague."

"Oh yes, *bubonic* – it produces buboes," interjected Henry.

"Do you know this from your knowledge of Latin or from your medical training?" I asked.

"Training?" questioned Henry.

"Yes, um, learning," I clarified.

"Oh, a bit of both."

"There is so much I could tell you to help if you will only listen and trust me," I pleaded as I leaned forward.

Suddenly I realised how desperate I sounded and that I was no longer the cool foreign traveller. Henry sat open mouthed as I regained my self-control.

"The most important thing for *everyone* to do is to clean the place and keep it clean," I continued, regaining control of the conversation.

"We are all clean in this household, even the surfs," Henry replied rather indignantly.

"I didn't mean any disrespect, Henry, but you don't understand bacteria."

"Bacteria?" questioned Henry.

"Yes, it is a Latin word."

"I can hear that, but what does it mean?"

"They are very little creatures, far too small to see, and they live inside our bodies and make us ill."

Henry seemed to try to suppress a little smile and asked, "What, like worms?"

"Yes, yes, exactly like worms, but much, much smaller."

"How can something so small make people ill and kill them?"

"Because there are millions and millions of them and our bodies need to develop white blood cells to fight them and this makes us ill," I tried to explain as simply as possible.

"White blood cells?" questioned Henry once more.

"Yes, they run through our bodies in our blood and fight bacteria. Once we have them, they can fight off the sickness, but only if it does not kill us before we grow these white blood cells."

Henry looked very confused now, but was no longer laughing. I waited a while for this to sink in. Finally Henry said, "So, if we get ill and don't die, we can survive any illness?"

"Er, no, it's not quite that simply. There are all sorts of bacteria that cause all sorts of different sicknesses. Our bodies need to develop different defences for all the different illnesses."

There was more silence as Henry thought. "So, if anyone survives the sickness once, they won't get it again?"

"It certainly makes it far less likely," I responded after a brief pause.

More silence followed until Henry said, "I have heard this about the pox."

Edmund was not sure if Henry meant chicken pox, small pox or syphilis but it didn't really matter and exclaimed, "Yes, yes! That is right. When a child gets the pox, he never gets it again."

More silence ensued and it lasted much longer this time as I tried to remain quiet. I remembered what my father used to say when he was selling something to a pharmacy customer, "You have two ears and one mouth, so say half as much as the other person if you are trying to sell something." I was trying to sell my ideas, so I did my best to keep quiet.

Eventually Henry expressed his next thought. "But people are always getting ill with a runny nose."

"Oh yes, this is true but when we get a cold, or a runny nose, it is never the same bacteria as the last cold." As I was saying this, I realised a cold is a virus and not bacteria, but I didn't think this was the best time to discuss the difference between a virus and a bacterium even if I were sure of the difference myself.

"So, what are the bacteria that are causing this sickness?" asked Henry as he began to put things in order in his head

I knew the answer to this one as I had found its name in my research before travelling. "This bacterium is called *yersinia pestis.*"

More silence followed and I could not resist adding, "And it is the worst bacterium in human history."

"Is this like the runny nose bacterium?" enquired Henry.

"No, it is always the same. Well, it changes very slowly, anyway."

"Changes?" asked Henry, feeling confused once more.

"Yes, the runny nose bacterium changes very quickly, so the cold you got last month is not the same bacterium that gave you a cold this month, but *yersinia pestis* remains the same, virtually."

Henry's face lit up like a light and he asked, "If the sickness has been around for ever, why do people still get it?"

"That's a very good question! It is because children who have not been immunised, will get it, which is why it recurs roughly every generation."

"Immunised?" enquired Henry, looking confused again.

"It means that because they have been exposed to the virus once, they are immune to it the next time."

"Have you been immunised, Edmund?"

I thought quickly and then answered, "When the sickness passed through Saxony, I may have caught a little bit of the sickness or I may just be lucky, but immunisation is not the only thing that will help avoid the sickness."

"Oh dear, this is getting too much!" exclaimed Henry feeling exasperated.

Fearing that I might lose Henry's attention, I thought it better to move on and said, "It is not so important to cure the sick but to avoid getting it in the first place."

Henry thought once more and asked, "Is it too late for Sister Cecelia who already has the sickness?"

At hearing this, I shivered as I had not realised anyone in Burford had actually got the Black Death. It was now my turn to be silent and eventually I said, "I do not know, but if you trust me, I will do my best to help you save her."

Henry smiled gently. Just then, there was a knock at the door.

"Come in," said Henry and the door opened to reveal Megan standing there with a frightened look on her face.

"Yes, what is it, Megan?"

"Scabbard has just come to tell Lord Burford that one of the sisters who was nursing Sister Cecelia has fallen ill as well."

12

The Council

I sat outside waiting whilst Henry was talking to his father. Despite his initial scepticism, Henry did seem to think there was something to what I had said about the sickness and he was now telling his father, who, of course, had the power to do something about it. But how would Lord Burford react? All these strange ideas that held no logic in their world.

As I sat, trying to be patient, I heard footsteps coming towards me and around the corner came Megan bearing a cup. I looked up and caught Megan's eye as she said, "I have brought you some beer, sir." The thought flashed through my mind that it was strange to have beer this early in the morning, but then I remembered that as there was no pure water, people drank beer because it was safer. "Thank you, Megan, that's very kind of you." I took the cup and Megan remained standing there. "Er, what brings you to Burford?" I asked, trying to think of something to say. As the last word left my lips, I remembered what Henry had told me about her parents' death.

"Oh, my parents were killed in Wales and one of the soldiers from Burford brought me back here. Since then, the lord has looked after me."

I felt embarrassed but tried not to show it as I wondered if the 'the lord' looking after her was meant to be Lord Burford or the Lord Jesus Christ?

"Oh, I see," I replied nervously and there was another uncomfortable silence.

Then Megan said, "I'm sure there are many things I could do to help around the town, but I am told to remain in the house where it is safer."

I looked at her for a moment and said, "Sit down." and shuffled along the bench to make room for her.

She sat nervously at the far end of the bench as I began to think of all the things she could help out with around the town.

"The most important thing in the short term is to clean up the town and get rid of anything that attracts rats, because rats are where the disease comes from."

"Rats? But rats are always with us! They sometimes attack babies, but they don't bring sickness."

This was clearly going to be difficult to explain, even to Henry and his father, let alone to an uneducated young girl. Could she even read?

Inside the room, Henry had outlined Edmund's ideas to his father and, of course, Lord Burford seemed very sceptical. However, young Henry had two powerful weapons on his side. First, he had been studying medicine at Oxford and second, he was Lord Burford's son and heir to the estate. On the other hand, not only did Lord Burford live in the middle ages – though, not in his mind – but he was also constrained by what was expected of him. He may be lord of the manor, but he was not free to think and do as he wished. I was aware of this and thought to myself, *Man is born free, but is everywhere in chains.* That concept would not be around for another few hundred years!

As Henry came to an end of what he had to say, his father sat silently looking a little perplexed and concerned.

Henry remained silent. He knew his father well and was aware that at times like this, it was best to leave his father to think in silence. Finally, Lord Burford broke his silence and asked, "What if all your friend's ideas are wrong?"

Henry thought carefully and replied, "I believe we would have little to lose as our present methods seem to be having little effect."

Silence followed once more until Lord Burford took a deep breath and said, "We shall call a council of the town and see what reaction we get."

After what seemed like hours but was probably no more than 30 minutes, I heard movement in the room I was seated outside. The door opened and Henry stood and looked at Megan and I. Megan jumped up immediately and gave a little curtsy.

I felt that Megan thought she was doing something wrong and felt the need to protect her, so I said, "I was just explaining to Megan about the rats."

Henry's eyes dropped from Megan to me and said, "Well, perhaps you would like to come in and explain more to my father."

I got up and Megan hurried away down the corridor.

As we entered the room, Lord Burford was standing and looking at us.

"Sit down, Edmund."

"Thank you," I said, trying to avoid any name or title as I was still not sure how to address the lord of the manor.

"Henry has explained your thoughts to me and there are a few questions I would like to ask."

"Okay."

"Eh?"

"I said it's all right. What can I tell you."

"First of all, what makes you think the rats bring the sickness?"

This was an easy question for me, as I had learnt about the Black Death in school as part of history lessons and also because I had studied Chaucer and the period he lived in.

"It's very simple really. The sickness started in the far east, near China, and is carried by fleas that get onto the rats. The rats get onto ships which go from port to port, and when the rats get off, that town then has the sickness. Soon it spreads out from there. The ships then move on to other ports and the sickness becomes a pandemic..."

"Pand?"

"Yes, pandemic. It means that it is everywhere."

"Oh, yes. Two Greek words put together."

I realised that Lord Burford could also speak Greek, or at least ancient Greek, and remembered that all the kings and queens of the past had been schooled in the classics, so I assumed any rich, educated person would also be. How strange that some could read and write in a dead, foreign language when the vast majority could not even read and write their own language.

"So, more rats get onto other ships and are taken to more ports and so the sickness has spread west and eventually reached England."

Lord Burford's face lighted up. This fitted in entirely with what he knew: that ships always carried rats and that the disease had spread across Europe and eventually probably landed on the south coast and spread up to Oxfordshire and Burford.

I sensed I was making progressed and went on. "It is not really the rats that are a big problem, but the sickness they carry with the fleas. We cannot get rid of the fleas, but we may be able to get rid of a lot of the rats."

"Henry tells me you suggest cats and dogs."

"Yes, the cats and dogs will kill some rats and frighten off others, but we also need to stop encouraging the rats to come into our houses."

"Encourage? How?"

"The rats can only live if we feed them by leaving around things they can eat."

"But all the granaries are on raised platforms to keep the rats out," Lord Burford explain in a rather perplexed voice.

I remembered the lovely little stone 'mushrooms' that I knew used to be used to put granaries on top so that the rats could not get the grain. "That is true, but whenever food is thrown into the street, the rats come and eat it. Rats cannot survive in such large numbers without help from humans who feed them."

"I think I understand."

"It's not just food, though. It's also the mess left by horses that encourage the rats. We must try to clear that up too."

I wasn't clear what term I should use for horse 'mess'. Should I call it manure, shit, or what? Mess seemed to do the trick, though.

"That could be a pretty big job," Lord Burford stated the obvious.

"Well, whatever we can do will help. It is also very important to keep everything around us clean and to keep on washing our hands."

"Why?";

"Because any bacteria on our hands make us ill and we pass that illness on when we touch others."

"Henry has told me you speak of 'bacteria'. What exactly is it?"

"They are tiny organisms that…"

"Organisms?"

"They are little animals that get into our bodies and make us ill."

"Oh, a bit like worms, you mean?"

"Yes, that is exactly right, like worms."

"But we have never seen these bacteria?"

"That's because they are far too small to see and there are millions of them in each body. The body makes little things to fight them, but this takes time and we may die before they have fought off the bacteria."

There was a long pause and Lord Burford asked, "How long does this take?"

"A few days, usually, but often the bacteria win the battle before they are killed."

Another silence ensued, and then he asked, "That is why, if a sick person survives a few days, they may well recover?"

"Yes, you are right, sir. Bacteria are everywhere, so we need to wash them off our hands and anything else we touch very frequently. It is also important to wash our food before we prepare it and to wash all things associated with food preparation."

"Mmm, it seems a little excessive to me."

"I assure you, it is completely necessary, sir."

It was now twice that I had used the term 'sir' and it did not seem to be the wrong thing to say. At this point, Henry made a rare interjection. "I have given a lot of thought to this concept of 'bacteria' and it does seem to make a lot of sense to me, Father."

Lord Burford's face became less sceptical. It was increasingly clear that Lord Burford put a lot of store in his son's thoughts, but whether this was because of what he said or because he was his son, he could not be sure. It was probably a bit of both.

I could see I was making progress with Lord Burford and left him to think for a while. I remembered once more what my father had told me: if I ever want to sell an idea, I should remember that I have two ears and one mouth, so I should listen twice as much as I speak. Finally, Lord Burford spoke. "I think there is much merit in what you say and Henry has pointed out that our current methods seem to have little effect, so we may as well try something else."

I took a deep breath and Lord Burford proceeded. "I will convene a council this afternoon and we will discuss the matter."

An hour later, Henry and I sat as Megan served us food before the council meeting that was to be held this afternoon. We two young men chatted easily as if we had known each other for years. Henry asked more questions and I did my best to explain without giving away the truth of how I knew all this, and where and what century I really came from. I kept reminding myself that no matter what Henry, his father, or anyone else thought of my strangeness, nothing could come anywhere close to the truth. As we ate, Megan was in and out at every opportunity, always giving me a big smile, so much so that I began to observe if she gave the same to Henry. I could see that she was polite and deferential towards him, but she did not give him the big smiles. Was she flirting with me? How should I react? Even though she was pretty, she was so dirty and her hair was matted. How was a high-class Norman lad meant to behave towards a low-class Welsh girl? Also, was Henry catching on to it?

After three courses, the meal seemed to be over. All courses had meat, meat and more meat. What I really wanted now, was a nice piece of cheesecake, but that didn't seem very likely. Even an apple would be nice! Soon we were both downstairs waiting for Lord Burford. The big door leading outside opened and Scabbard appeared. His eyes scanned the entrance hall and then he said, "Oh, I just

came to tell His Lordship we are all ready for the council."
Just then, Lord Burford appeared and Scabbard repeated,
"We are all ready for the council, sir."

"Thank you, Scabbard, we are leaving now."

The party walked out of Burford House, down the
road, across the river and into the church. Upon entering, all
those waiting stood up and gave a little bow. The church of
St. John the Baptist was always on the Decovny family
tourist route for any visitor so, even if it wasn't during a
service, I had been in it a few times. When the Burford
party approached, others entering held back. All who
entered dipped their fingers into holy water and crossed
themselves, and I found himself following without thinking
what I was doing. I looked at the murky mess left behind
and thought of all the bacteria in there that could enter
someone's body through a cut or when one's fingers came
in contact with one's mouth. As I entered, I was conscious
that it was smaller than I remembered. At the front there
was room for a large table around which a number of
dignitaries were seated.

I wondered if this council was like a king's council
where they did what they were told or whether it was like a
Carterton town council where things were debated and free
conclusions reached. As soon as Lord Burford began to
speak, it became clear that he was in charge. Soon he
introduced me as a traveller from the east of Europe where
the sickness had already passed through and a lot had been
learnt. The council deferentially sat in virtual silence, but
there were a few intakes of breath as Lord Burford
explained about the rats and their fleas. When he asked for
messages to be sent out to all surrounding villages for any
dogs and cats to be brought into the town, there was much
shuffling and murmuring as the priest indicated he wished
to speak. He was the only council member brave enough to
open his mouth and showed that although Lord Burford

was in charge, he did not have total control. The priest asked, "My Lord, did Pope Gregory IV not declare the association between Satan, witches and cats a century ago?"

"Indeed, he did, Father, but God has put all animals on this Earth for our benefit and so cats must be here for a reason. Perhaps we have so far not realised God's purpose for cats."

"Yes, Your Lordship, I am sure that cats do have their uses for God, but I am also sure that if God wanted us to, er, welcome cats into our community, he would have told us so."

"I am sure that he would have done so, but we may have missed his purpose. Perhaps cats have become the Devil's agents only because we have not set them to God's purpose before?"

The priest was silenced and I realised Lord Burford had given this a lot of thought and was ready for any objections. It also became clear that the whole exercise would not be as easy as I had hoped. The people of 14th century Burford were not going to welcome my greater 21st century knowledge with open arms and overwhelming thanks.

Lord Burford moved on to talk about the need to clean the streets and remove anything that may attract rats. A site would be established just outside the town for dry rubbish and any waste food was to be cast into the river. I nearly fell off my seat at hearing this, but realised that with no municipal dustmen, there was little alternative. I decided that I would later ask Lord Burford to set it up downriver from the town, away from where fresh water would be drawn from the river for washing and drinking. Let the people of Witney get cholera! As for the two nuns who had already contracted the disease, they were to be nursed by the same volunteering nuns and all others were to be kept away from them.

I listened carefully to check whether the lord had left anything out and was relieved when he started to talk about the frequent washing of hands, cleaning of all work surfaces, especially in the kitchen, and washing all food before it was prepared. Once more the priest indicated his desire to speak and this time he looked even more disapproving than over the cats. Lord Burford nodded to the priest to speak. "This sounds very Semitic to me." He seemed to spit out the word 'Semitic'.

"The Jews do many things the same way in which we do it, or in similar ways, and they also do some things that we may not always do. It is not their actions that render them unacceptable to God, but their rejection of Christ. We all here accept the truth of the Lord Jesus Christ and that the only way to Heaven is through Christ and his only holy church."

The priest gave a benign smile, lowered his head and said, "My Lord."

Once more I realised how much thought the lord had given this matter and how cleverly he had silenced his most powerful objector.

As the meeting was coming to a close, Lord Burford told the council that his instructions were to be carried out and that most of the detail would be overseen by young Henry, Edmund de Covny and Scabbard. He finishing with, "Thank you, gentlemen. I am sure..."

At this point, I suddenly interrupted with, "Oh, and get rid of that water in the church entry or keep changing it."

At this, the priest jumped up and exclaimed, "This really is too much, *My* Lord! He speaks as if holy water is just... well, er, just water!"

"Of course holy water is pure and will always remain pure. I am sure de Covny was not referring to the water in the font, *were* you de Covny?"

"No, My Lord, I meant it was, er, er..."

"Good. Just a misunderstanding. We shall start first thing tomorrow morning, but you are all to start spreading my instructions immediately."

The lord's face was stone cold and as white as a sheet as he walked towards the door. The council members bowed and Henry followed his father out with me close behind him. My head was racing and the only consolation I could find, was that I had at least mindlessly followed the others in dipping his finger and crossing myself. How much worse things would be if I had been seen not doing what all good Christians would do and if I'd never seen how those in the Catholic Church of the 21st century, who still habitually maintained the crossing ritual, were conditioned and compelled to mindlessly follow this ritual. The consequences of not doing so would mean social exclusion at the very least. In the 14th century it would probably mean being burned the stake. The walk back to Burford House was in silence. Once back inside, Lord Burford disappeared and Henry indicated that I was to follow him. We went into a room and Henry closed the door. Then he turned towards me. "What did you think you were doing?"

"I'm sorry. I should have chosen my words more carefully."

"Chosen them more carefully? What made you say such a thing at all?"

I kept my mouth shut.

"Apart from what you said, you should not have spoken at all without permission from the lord."

"Yes, I know, Henry. I don't know what came over me."

"My father is trying his best to help you and what do you do?"

I remained silent.

"My father may be lord of the manor, but he can't be seen challenging the teaching of the church. You could have done irreparable harm to what…"

At this point, there was a knock at the door and Henry bit his tongue before saying, "Come in."

The door opened and Scabbard stood there with an expressionless face. "Lord Burford commands to see Edmund de Covny."

I froze as Henry remained silent and averted his gaze.

After a few seconds, I found the strength to walk towards the door and followed Scabbard out and along the corridor. My mind was racing. What would Lord Burford say? What would he do? For the first time since I was 'captured', I wished I had stayed at home. A few minutes ago I felt like a great prophet and now I felt like Judas.

The walk through the house seemed like a long walk to the gallows. Eventually we came to a door and Scabbard knocked. "Come," came the voice of Lord Burford through the door. Scabbard opened the door and indicated that I should go in. As I did, Scabbard closed the door behind me.

"I   am   sorry,   Lord   Bur…"

"Sit down, Edmund," Lord Burford cut me off forcefully.

There was a long silence and then he said, "My son and heir is very taken with your thoughts and I can see much merit in them, but you must see that some may find them strange and frightening. Others may even find them threatening."

"Yes, sir."

"You must know that your ideas have no power without my endorsement. You must learn to say nothing without first expressing it to me or Henry."

"Yes, My Lord. I cannot express my remorse for my foolhardy behaviour."

There was another silence. Then he said, "As you come from a far off land, you may have different customs but you must remember where you are. Go now. Have a good evening with Henry and we shall start early in the morning."

"Yes, My Lord. Thank you."

13

The Music Room

As I walked back to where I had left Henry, the full enormity of my situation was dawning on me. No longer was I on a little adventure from which it was easy to return. I was now caught in a time from which I could not return easily. I was so far from my laptop and I could hardly just walk out of the town. Irrespective of trying to explain my situation to the people who now knew me in the 14th century, there were guards at all the exits from the town who would prevent my exit. They may be there to stop people coming in, but how would I be able to get past them without having to explain why I wanted to leave and where I was going?

There was the sound of a flute that got louder as I approached the room where I had left Henry. On reaching the room, I knocked and heard Henry's voice say, "Come."

Opening the door with some trepidation, I was greeted with a broad smile from Henry who ushered me in and gestured to a seat. As I sat down, I noticed the flute in Henry's hand. He held it up and asked, "Do you play?"

"Er, well, not really, but I can play a little on the keyboard, usually with only one hand."

"Keyboard?"

Realising that I had made another period mistake, I decided to adopt another approach and create the impression that I would expect Henry to know what a keyboard was.

"Yes, you know, where you press a note on a board and it causes a little hammer to hit different strings that ring on different notes."

"Oh, you mean like the new form of dulcimer?"

"Yes, sort of, but the hammer is moved by a mechanism that is operated when the note is pressed."

"I see! Come with me," said Henry as he jumped up and headed for the door.

I followed Henry through the house to parts I had not been to before. As we walked, I thought there had been no mention of what Henry's father had to say about what had been said in the church. Why was this? Was he too embarrassed to raise the subject? Had Lord Burford told his son that he was going to give me a bollocking and that would be all? But when would he have said this? He had had no time alone with his father. Was it that he knew his father so well and knew that he would merely express his opinion and leave it at that? Was Lord Burford's forgiveness just because he, Edmund, was now Henry's new friend? Was it just because Henry was impressed with what I had to say and because Henry was medically educated that his father too thought there must be merit in what I had to say?

Making our way through the house was a long labyrinth of corridors and doors until we reached a 'staircase', except that it wasn't a proper staircase, but really just a ladder up to the next floor. Henry bounded up it and I followed as we passed along another corridor. Eventually Henry turned into what was obviously a music room. I had been in music rooms at school but had never seen one in someone's house. All around us were musical instruments, some of which I recognised, others that I had no concept at all of what they might be or what sound they might make.

Henry moved across the room to one instrument saying, "Here you are, a dulcimer. I think this is what you mean by a key board!"

Moving towards the instrument and looking at it, I said, "Yes, but a keyboard is more complicated."

Henry picked up a couple of sticks and began to play but, of course, it was not a tune I knew and not in a time signature I recognised.

"The dulcimer is usually played with a bow, but this new form of dulcimer is becoming popular. Now you play," Henry said as he passed me the sticks.

What could I say or do? I had played a xylophone before and that wasn't too difficult, so I'll try, but what to play? Something traditional and not too modern; something nice and easy in C. I made a few random strokes with the hammers to find out where the notes where before saying, "I have never played a dulcimer before but I will try." Then I began to knock out 'Auld Lang Syne'.

Henry's face was a mixture of puzzlement and pleasure at his friend's musical production. "Is that a tune from your country?"

"Yes, we sing it each New Year."

"Why?"

"I don't know, it's just a tradition." Obviously that old tune was not old enough.

"Oh. Anything else?" enquired Henry.

I thought for a few moments and then tentatively started to play 'Greensleeves', thinking that if it were not written by Henry VIII, it may be a little older and Henry Burford might just recognise it. He didn't seem to recognise it, but then Henry put out his hands to take the hammers and moved around to the other side of the instrument and began to play. Out came 'Greensleeves', but as a very augmented version. I smiled and exclaimed, "Oh, you know this tune!"

"No, I just heard what you were playing." I then understood that Henry was a very good musician.

Realising that any further attempts at playing myself would merely add to my embarrassment, I listened to Henry playing various pieces and then, looking around the room at all the other instruments, I asked, "Would you tell me a little about all these other instruments? Some I don't recognise."

Henry looked pleased and turned to the nearest instrument, which had a round pear-shaped body, and began to bow it. "This is a rebec."

"A rebec? We have something very similar called a violin but it makes a different sound."

Putting it down, Henry then picked up another instrument which seemed to be a cross between a harp and a violin and began to produce a strange sound. "This is called a psaltery but it's not very easy to play."

"So I see," I said, looking around at other instruments and my eyes lighted up as I saw what looked like a recorder. Picking it up I began to play what I believed was an Irish jig that I didn't know the name of. Henry picked up a flute and joined in as if he had been playing the tune all his life. Once more I was very impressed. Then Henry picked up an extremely strange looking instrument that had many different strings and as many tuning pegs in many different places.

"This is a nyckelharpa," Henry explained with a proud tone to his voice.

"Is it really?" I exclaimed.

"Yes. It's a traditional Swedish instrument and extremely difficult to play. We haven't had it for long and Father has commissioned a Swedish troubadour who lives in London to come and teach me how to play it."

Henry put down the nyckelharpa very reverentially and said with a sigh, "So I won't try to play it now as I have little idea how to start."

At this point, there was a knock at the door and again Megan was there with some food. On entering, Megan looked at me and said, "Lord and Lady Burford send their apologies for not having a family meal tonight but they are both very busy."

"Oh, please tell them I am happy with this and I thank them for their hospitality."

Once more, Megan was very chatty and full of big smiles for me. Henry sat almost silently and grinning as he watched Megan and I flirt. I was beginning to warm to Megan and see the beauty behind the grime. Even so, I did wince a bit when she reached past me and I could smell her odour. I would have liked to chat her up, but did not know how to behave towards a servant girl in medieval society when I came from a society that did not really have servants any more. Even if I did know what to do, it was impossible with Henry sitting in the corner smirking. Eventually Megan ran out of excuses to stay and left with a little curtsy.

As the evening progressed and we munched through the food, mainly some sort of bread and cakes with cheese, I cut the cheese with a knife and ripped the bread with my teeth as I became aware that Henry was giving me funny looks.

"What?" I asked.

Henry was obviously fully aware of what I meant as he immediately said,

"Why do you eat your food like that?"

"Like what?"

"Biting into it like an animal would," Henry explained with obvious distaste.

"Well, how else would I eat it?"

"Like a human being and not like a base animal."

I suddenly realised I had committed a totally unacceptable social 'no-no' and just looked at Henry for guidance.

After a couple of seconds, Henry smiled and said, "Like this." He was holding up a piece of cheese between his thumb and forefinger of his left hand whilst he held the bread with his other fingers against the base of his thumb. He then used his knife to cut a piece of bread and then a piece of cheese before he popped it into his mouth.

I followed his example and Henry smiled, saying rather patronisingly, "Well done! I assume the other way is how the people of Saxony would eat?"

"Yes!" I exclaimed, thankful for some excuse for my taboo behaviour.

"Well, here even the most lowly surf would not eat like an animal."

Oh my god, I thought with a mixture of shame, bemusement and relief at the realisation it could have been so much worse had I eaten like that in front of the rest of the Burford family or the peasants and surfs of Burford.

I felt very embarrassed but soon the conversation moved on. As the meal came to an end, Henry proceeded to play me more instruments I did not know such as a viol, clearly an early viola played on the lap or between the knees, and a set of bagpipes which apparently was usually only played by poor people as it could be made from reed pipes and the bag from goatskin. After many good tunes from Henry and a few painful noises from me, Henry picked up a strange looking object with a handle he began to turn and produced a rasping sound. *"What is that?"* I asked in amazement.

"It's called a hurdy-gurdy."

"Oh, I have heard of a hurdy-gurdy but never seen one and definitely never heard one."

As Henry tried to teach me to play the instrument, it began to get dark outside. I thought it must now be about 9:30 pm on a midsummer's night and another obvious observation occurred to me: there was no form of artificial light other than candles, and why use them during midsummer when it was only dark for 6 hours? It was just about enough time to sleep. Another obvious problem suddenly occurred to me: where was I to sleep? I had no idea where I would retire and no idea how to broach the subject. I just hoped Henry would tell me.

Soon the evening drew to a halt and Henry put down the hurdy-gurdy. "I will show you to your room."

"Oh, thank you, Henry."

I followed Henry upstairs once more and when we came to a door, he asked, "Do you want to go in there first?"

Hesitantly, I pushed open the door to reveal what I assumed was a privy, mainly by the smell. *Oh thank God*, I thought, because although the day had been full of excitement and despite having had little to drink, I was now busting for a pee. Inside was a stone chair with a hole in it that seemed to overhang the house to the outside. Having had a long wee I turned to the sink – what sink? So I walked out to where Henry was still waiting.

Once more I followed Henry until we came to a room with the door ajar. As we walked in, I saw a room that was quite large for a guest room, with a big bed in the middle. This was obviously not a servant's room. Henry turned to leave, then stopped and paused before saying, "I know my father spoke to you, so that is finished with, but do you mind if I ask you one thing?"

"No, not at all," I replied, fearful of what was to come.

"From my knowledge of medicine you talk a lot of sense, but I cannot understand why you think *holy* water could ever be harmful?"

"I, er, wasn't thinking straight whilst in the council meeting."

Henry nodded in silence, turned once more and closed the door behind himself.

It became clear to me that no matter how intelligent, 'educated' and open-minded Henry was, he was still a product of his society and time so he did actually believe holy water was something other than ordinary water. Climbing into bed I could feel some of the feathers sticking through the bed and the pillows. However, it was quite comfortable and seemed pretty clean. I lay awake for a while reflecting on the strangest day in my life and wondering if I would ever be able to return to the 21st century. That was the last conscious thought I had and the eventful day soon had its inevitable effect – sleep.

14

Breakfast

I was woken by a loud knock and as I woke up, I automatically called out,

"Come in."

The door opened and Scabbard was standing there.

"I am sorry to wake you, sir, but it is morning and breakfast is prepared."

I looked at Scabbard, in shock, not realising where I was or who this man was. A second later it all came flooding back to him.

"Oh, thank you, Scabbard."

I noticed a bowl in Scabbard's hands and he placed it next to the bed. Looking at it I could see there was water in it. Then Scabbard dropped a cloth next to the bowl, saying, "For you, sir."

Scabbard turned to leave and my head went back onto the pillow. Yes, I was awake and it hadn't all been a dream. I really was still in the 14th century, in a large house five miles and 7 centuries from where I should have been sleeping.

Quickly I jumped out of bed and found my clothes on the floor where I had dropped them after the long day yesterday. As I had brought nothing to change into with me, there was no other choice than to wear them again. This reminded me that I had not planned to be in this present position. A planned short exploration had turned into an adventure the outcome of which was completely unknown. Had it been a good idea to travel again? We shall see! I had a quick wash in the water, which was warm at least, and put on my clothes.

I went down the stairs to where Megan was waiting to show me into the breakfast room. "Good morning, Megan."

"Good morrow, sir. Did you sleep well?"

"Yes, very well, thank you."

"My Lord is waiting for you," she said as she opened the door.

"Ah, Edmund," said Lord Burford, indicating a chair to sit on.

"Good morning, sir."

"Good morrow."

"Good morrow, Henry," I replied, picking up on the socially expected terminology.

At this point, I noticed Scabbard was standing a little away from the table as if waiting to serve. "Good morrow, Scabbard."

"Good morrow, sir."

This was not the same room as we had eaten in before. It faced east so that the midsummer morning sun streamed into the room. It was a real breakfast room.

Soon the door opened again and in walked Megan with a tray laden with food. She was followed by an old woman also carrying a tray.

"Ah, thank you, Megan and Rachael. Edmund, this is Rachael, the housekeeper," Lord Burford said.

"Good morrow, sir," Rachael said. Then she turned to Edmund. "I am pleased to be of service to you." She finishing with a curtsy.

At least, that's what I thought she said, because her accent was even stronger than the Burfords'. Even Megan was easier to understand with her medieval Welsh accent.

"Thank you, Rachael," I replied with a nod, not really knowing what the social etiquette was towards a housekeeper in the 14th C..

The two left the room and I couldn't help but think Megan had not been at all flirtatious in the presence of Lord Burford. Or maybe it was the presence of the housekeeper. Maybe both.

Following the lead of the Burfords, I got stuck into breakfast, this time being even more careful to watch for the eating etiquette of the 14th century. I wouldn't want them thinking I was lower than the lowest surf! There were various sorts of bread, warm milk, probably fresh from the cow, what smelt like fish and, of course, meat, meat and a little more meat. *Don't these people ever eat any fruit or vegetables?* Their turds must be like bricks! My father could make a fortune selling senokots to them, and lots of haemorrhoid cream too. Mind you, having seen, and smelt, the privy last night, it was hardly surprising that the people of the 14th century tried to defecate as little as possible.

It quickly became obvious that this was clearly a working breakfast and soon Lord Burford asked, "Well, Edmund, where do you suggest we start today?"

"Okay, I have thought about this and it's probably best if we start with Burford House." I stopped here to check their reaction, because I was aware that I was suggesting the place needed cleaning up.

"What would you do?" enquired the lord

"First of all, we will go to the kitchen. Let me look around and see what's needed. Then perhaps we can do something with the privy."

There was a pause and Lord Burford looked at Edmund, so he thought he had better take the lead. "I have told you about little bacteria that make people ill and the present sickness is just one particular sort of bacteria that is more dangerous than others, but any sort of sickness will make the sufferer ill and, therefore, far more likely to succumb to the Black Death when it comes along. We will all be more resilient towards that sickness if we don't have any other sort of sickness. These little bacteria grow in all sorts of places and then get into our bodies where they make us ill and weak. Because we are weak, the Black Death has a greater chance of killing us when it comes along. If we eliminate as many places as possible where bacteria can grow, then we will all be much healthier."

"I see, but if these bacteria are so small that we cannot see them, how do you know they are there?"

"Good question!" I had thought about this one and decided to tell him something close to the truth. "If you look through glass," I said as I looked through the window glass that was not perfect, "sometimes things become distorted and sometimes what you are looking at becomes bigger." I paused for confirmation.

"Yeees."

"If the glass is made carefully, then things can be made to look much bigger. If that glass is put at the one end of a tube and another glass is put at the other end of the tube, then it is possible to see things that are very, very small."

"I see."

"This tube is also very good for looking at the stars."

"I suppose it would be. What is this tube called?"

"For looking at small things, it is called a microscope. For looking at the stars, it is called a telescope."

"Ah, yes. 'Small' for looking at little things and 'distance' to look at the stars."

It now became clear again that Lord Burford could also speak Greek. I suppose he would, being an educated lord.

Never mind the fact that he thinks water can have magical qualities if it's blessed, just as long as he can speak Greek!

"But tell me, do they have these tubes in Saxony?"

I realised I needed to be careful and replied, "Yes, but not very many. They are difficult to make and very expensive."

"And was it invented by a Saxon?"

I felt a little gremlin get onto my shoulder and told Lord Burford, "No, it was invented by an Italian called Galileo."

"Mmm, a clever man."

"Oh, not really; he thought the Earth went around the sun and not that the sun goes around the Earth."

A little chuckle was heard from Henry and his father.

After a long silence, I moved things on to say, "Then we shall go over to the abbey to see if there is anything we can do for the sick nuns."

I knew this would be very dangerous for my own health and that it would be better to stay away, but I knew I had to try to do something. "This is a very risky thing to do, so I think I should be the only one to enter their sick room."

Silence filled the room. Then Henry said, "Father, I would like to accompany Edmund in anything he has to do."

More silence ensued.

"All right, but you must not do anything more than is absolutely necessary." Lord Burford seemed to be caught between wanting to protect his son, needing him to be able to behave like a man and not just the lord's son, and knowing the public image of the Burford family was important.

"Something that would be helpful is very fine muslin." Not knowing if muslin was around in the 14th century I just hoped for the best.

"Yes, we can arrange that, but what for."

"The bacteria enter our bodies mainly through the mouth and nose, so if we can filter this out, it may help us to avoid catching the disease. We need to have it layer upon layer and made in such a way that it can be tied around the mouth and nose."

"Oh, and filled with flower petals against the stink," the lord added helpfully.

I had a picture in my head of the Black Death of 1665 with a man wearing a pointed face mask with petals in the nose piece.

"No, a ring of roses won't really help. The smell of flowers doesn't help other than to cover up the smell. The muslin is just to filter the bacteria."

"That sounds like a job for Megan, Scabbard."

"Yes, sir, I shall instruct her."

Now I realised why Scabbard was there: to hear what was required and ensure instructions were carried out. I had wondered why he sat there not eating, and had felt a little rude eating in front of someone who was not, but I suppose a servant is used to that.

By now nearly all the food was consumed and Lord Burford wiped his mouth with a cloth napkin. At this, Scabbard walked towards the door and disappeared for a few moments before returning. I assumed Scabbard had done this a thousand times before and knew the signals for the end of the meal. During the silence I asked,

"What is happening with the street cleaning?"

Lord Burford's eyes moved towards Scabbard who said, "All is in hand, sir, and should already have started."

It became clear that Lord Burford had started giving instructions the night before when Henry and I were in the music room. They seemed to work well together.

At that moment, the door opened and in walked the cook and Megan who began to clear the table. Soon the strange work in the strange time would start and I remembered something I had forgotten to ask for before. "Oh yes, Lord Burford, we need to dig a rubbish pit."

"A what?"

"A pit, or a hole, to put all the rubbish in."

"Oh, a hole for the garbage," interpreted the lord, translating my words to 14th century terminology.

"Yes, somewhere outside the town."

"Well, we usually burn most of it and a lot goes into the river."

"Burning is good, but dumping garbage into the river is not because it poisons the water we have to drink," I explained.

"We can get drinking water upstream and dump the garbage downstream."

I paused and cogitated on this logic before saying, "That means we get the poison from upstream and poison other people downstream."

"There are few people upstream and Witney is outside our jurisdiction," the lord said logically.

There was another pause whilst I thought of a way to deal with this one. "The garbage will poison the water and the fish we eat from the water, so we all need to ensure that others don't get poisoned to ensure we don't get poisoned."

Lord Burford looked a little bemused and then shrugged and said, "All right, if you think it's necessary I will issue instruction that garbage is not to be dumped in the river under any circumstances."

During this exchange, the table had been cleared by Megan and Cook and as they were leaving the room, Lord Burford said, "Megan, you are aware you will be assisting these men today?"

Megan turned and with her best little-girl-smile said, "Oh yes, My Lord. I know I am to do whatever they ask of me."

"Good girl." Megan and Cook departed with their laden trays.

Lord Burford's face now went solemn as he said, "So, we're off to the church first where a special mass will be said for our work today."

I tried my best to prevent my face from showing the horror I suddenly felt. What is a *special mass*? I would be expected to go, of course, and how should I behave? I must keep my mouth shut and act as if I take it all seriously! Finally, I stammered, "Oh, er, yes, of course, sir."

15

The Special Mass

As we approached the church along with the full Burford House entourage, my mind was racing as to how to deal with this new test. I had already messed things up big time over religion and for not knowing what all medieval people would know, and now I was to face a bigger test. My heart was in my mouth as we entered the church where I recently nearly ruined it all.

The priest welcomed Lord Burford and it became clear this was not for the whole town but just for the Burford household. But what was a special mass? In fact, when was a mass not special? My mind sprang back to all my Religious Education lessons at school and how Catholics don't just go to church, but that they have to go to mass where it seems they get a special sort of magic they cannot get without going to mass. In fact, it seems that if they don't get what ever it is they get from a mass, they think they will go to Hell. I remembered the class being in raptures of disbelief when this came up in Religious education.. What did they get from a mass that they could not get anywhere else? Surely this was just a sales technique to get people to go to church, by frightening them with the consequences of not going? It's just like those online con merchants who try to convince people that if they don't send thousands of pounds to an account, they will miss out on the opportunity of millions. Surely even a medieval mind could see through that little gimmick?

The priest turned to the altar and began speaking in what sounded like Latin, but it did not quite resemble the little Latin I knew. I assumed this was what they called 'Church Latin', but why God would need a different sort of Latin, or any different sort of language? Surely if they believe God is omniscient then he knows all languages, so why would medieval English not suffice? I had learnt about the Second Vatican Council, known as the Vatican II, which apparently allowed people to talk to their God in their own language, but that was not till 1967 – over 600 years from where I was now. What had confused me in the lesson was why people needed permission from an earthly being to do this?

As I watched the priest wave his arms about and talk with his back to the congregation, all the other bits of my Religious Education lessons came to mind, and when those around me started to chant, I easily mumbled along with them at the right time. I remembered that a special mass had to be paid for, which seemed very strange behaviour for any sort of *god*. Then I remembered the Counter-Reformation which was apparently an answer to Luther and his followers who criticised the Roman Catholic Church for selling indulgencies and forgiveness. That would have to wait another few hundred years to happen as well, but at the moment they still charged to get God's favour.

Then the memory of going to a midnight mass a couple of years ago with a Catholic friend, Gerry, sprang into my mind, and I remember being so disappointed that there was no sing-along. It was just a professional choir that people listened to. In front of me, pasted on the back of the next pew, there had been a plaque that read, 'Pray for the family of Timothy Leary' or who ever. I had asked Gerry why they should pray specifically for any particular person, or their families, and what praying does. Gerry had been very reluctant to talk about his beliefs and I had assumed this had been because he was embarrassed when he put his beliefs into words for someone who had not been conditioned into his belief system. Then I had had a vision of a book I had seen on a shelf in my house and wondered if it may answer some questions. There it was: a bright yellow book entitled *The complete idiot's guide to Catholicism.* I had picked it out and over the next few weeks, with growing astonishment, waded through what *all* Catholics – no matter of personal choice here – *had* to believe.

Apparently, if he did not go to mass once a week and on holy days, he would have a break with his relationship with his God and he would have to go to Hell. I did ask Gerry why God would send him to Hell just for not going through some ritual, but he seemed to have no idea. In fact, he knew very little about the doctrine of Catholicism and even less about why things were a certain way. As for the 'history', or the Bible, he knew virtually nothing. Even more surprisingly, it soon became clear he did not want to know. So why was he such an avid Catholic? Gerry claimed he was not an avid Catholic. So why did he always go to mass once a week and on holy days? Gerry had no answer to this either. It seems he just did it because everyone around him and in his family did so, and no one ever said no!

When I was in the church with Gerry I noticed that on the back of the bench in front of us was a plaque saying, 'Pray for the family of Timothy Leary' and I had asked Gerry why people should pray for Timothy Leary and his family, rather than any other family, but got no answer. Then it occurred to me that the commandment to pray was there because the family of Timothy Leary had *paid* to have the plate put there. A 'contribution to the church' I think would be the term used by these victims of the con merchants to have the plate put there in the belief that if people prayed for them, they would get extra 'points' in Heaven and would have to spend less time in Purgatory: a concept for which there was no biblical reference at all and had been completely made up as had the concept of a 'sacred heart'. As Timothy Leary's family had paid for the plaque, what was the difference between that and paying to buy an indulgence in pre-Counter-Reformations times? Not a lot, really!

The book did not say so, but I remembered how in a Religious Education discussion it had been observed that the Greeks and Romans believed that there was a family of gods floating in the sky and how, when the Romans took over the Christian sect, they had simply grafted Christianity onto these traditional beliefs. The father of the gods, Zeus, became God the father and his wife, Hera, became Mary the mother of God. The children of the gods had their roles filled by the son of God, Jesus. As for the lesser gods, it seemed that they were now referred to as the saints. The commandment, 'Thou shall have but one God' could thus be compatible in their minds with worshipping the different variations of these gods. There was general consensus within the student group of this analysis, but the Religious Education teacher, Miss Priest – yes, that really was her name – didn't seem to be very comfortable with this analysis. In fairness, though, she was happy for us to discuss the matter and express any views we wanted. Something that would not likely to be tolerated in the 14th century. Come to think of it, would it be tolerated in a Catholic school in the 21st century? Looking around the church at the very beautiful stained-glass windows, the models of Mary and the crucified Jesus, not to mention the gold and royal standards, I remembered that the 'Ten'

Commandments were actually 17 for the Protestant churches and in the original Hebrew, but only 16 commandments for the Catholic Church. They, very conveniently, left out 'Thou shall not worship graven images'. If you take graven images out of the Catholic faith, there wouldn't be much left!

At the time of studying Gerry's beliefs – but were they really *his* beliefs – I had just looked into the subject because Gerry was my friend and as a matter of interest, but now I was in a situation where this knowledge was vital. Even though I had opened my big mouth before, I did realise the necessity to know how to play the game. Having had some insight into the Catholic faith in the 21st century, I had some idea of how much stronger, and less questioned, the same beliefs were nearly 700 years earlier. This was before the age of the Enlightenment, and before any scientific analysis of the temporal world, let alone the spiritual world. I doubted if anyone in this church, or in the whole of Burford, questioned that their mumblings might not be listened to by anyone except those in the church. Whilst I could understand that people living before the age of Enlightenment might have believed such nonsense, having had personal experience of the workings of the medieval mind, I was becoming increasingly bemused as to how *anyone* in the 21st century could possibly be taken in by such illogical beliefs. Every time this thought entered my head, I reminded myself never to show any incredulity. I remembered the price to pay for heresy was to be burnt at the stake. I did not fancy myself as a latter day Ridley or Lattimer. Latter day, or was it future day?

Suddenly the whole congregation began reciting the Lord's prayer. I knew this and could join in enthusiastically. I got to the bit about 'as we forgive them who trespass against us' and carried on with 'for thine...' but realised no one else was following me. Then I remembered that the bit 'For thine is the kingdom, the power and the glory, forever and ever, amen', had been added by Henry VIII who didn't think God's version – as Christians would see it – was good enough. Henry VIII had added it but I could not understand why the Church of England kept it nearly 400 years later. So, Henry had separated the English church from the Roman church, but that was no reason for keeping in his addition centuries later. Either God was right or he needed to have his thoughts added to by mere mortals. Surely it makes a mockery of the word of God?

It was now clear that the service was over and all started to exit the church. It seems there had been no obvious conflicts between my behaviour and what was expected of me. Even the 'for thine...' insertion seemed to have gone unnoticed. I had got away with it! We all exited the church and made our way over the bridge, up the hill and into Burford House. I had passed another test and now the job of helping the people of Burford to avoid the worst of the Black Death could commence.

16

The Kitchen

There was no time to waste and as soon as we were back at Burford House, Scabbard joined us as Lord Burford bid farewell and left the task to Henry and me. The first visit would be to the house kitchen.

Scabbard opened the door and ushered us in. There, lined up, as if awaiting a royal visit, were all the kitchen staff and the rest of the house staff. Cook stepped forward and gave a little curtsy.

"Good day, sirs."

"Good day, Cook," replied Henry.

"Good day, Cook," I followed now that I was clear on how to address her.

I looked along the line and there was Megan who seemed to give me a knowing smile, but that was probably just my imagination. Then my eyes moved around the large kitchen; the largest room in the house. The first thought that struck me was that it was covered in more grease than John Travolta! It was *everywhere*. Oh dear! How to explain this?

Not wanting to jump in straight away with what would probably be seen as criticism, I started to move around the kitchen. As I moved past a smaller table at the edge of the room, there was a sudden 'whoosh' and I saw what seemed to be a black shadow move from a corner to under a large oven. I jumped a little and exclaimed, "What was that?"

"Oh, don't you worry about that, sir. Them ain't rats: them's just cockroaches," reassured Cook.

Pulling myself together I thought, *Oh well, that's all right, then. It's only a swarm of cockroaches anyway.* I shivered and then remembered being told that some of the best hotels in London still had cockroaches in the second half of the 20th century.

Moving around the kitchen I noticed the tables looked clean, but how clean? Moving on to the pots and pans, I could see they had all been washed but they still seemed to be covered in a thin film of grease. Well, with no fairy liquid, what else can be expected? They were obviously cleaning where they could, but *the floor* was in a sorry state! It was covered in bits of food. What rat could resist this? What to do? How could this be explained without upsetting too many people too much? Remembering I had been given the authority of Lord Burford, I decided to explain things before I gave instructions.

Turning to the still assembled domestic household, who were still standing in silence and unmoving, I moved around the kitchen and began to explain things.

"Rats only live where humans provide food and warmth for them. Before humans came onto the Earth, there were virtually no rats. They only thrive because we provide food and housing for them." I paused for a while for this to sink in. As I was about to proceed, I became aware that Scabbard wanted to speak.

"Yes, Scabbard, what is it?"

"Well, surely before God put us on the Earth there was nothing else? He only put the rats and other creatures here for us after he had made us."

Oh dear, here we go again. This time, however, it seemed no big deal. Thinking quickly I said, "He only created two of us at first, so as the population grew, we made life easier for the rats and their population grew as well."

"Oh, I see," said Scabbard, who seemed satisfied.

Moving the conversation back to what was needed, I said, "So, what we need to do is to ensure there is as little food as possible available for them to eat. Therefore, we must make sure there is nothing at all for them to eat. This means that no food at all must be allowed to fall onto the floor, or if it is, then it must be cleared up immediately. Any stored food must be kept out of reach of any rats that may be around."

As I paused, Cook said, "Er, excuse me, sir, but we already do that. All the flour pots and meat barrels are on these stands, sir." She pointed to a large barrel-shaped container on a raised platform.

"This is very good, Cook. I'm very pleased to see it. It just means no waste must ever be left behind, especially last thing at night."

Cook straightened herself up and beamed with pride. I realised I would get furthest by complimenting her and the staff, so I added, "I think we're going to get on very well working together, Cook."

Cook beamed more and I took the opportunity to add, "And I can see you make sure the tables are kept very clean too, so it is only important that you make sure they are cleaned every night with water, and once a week with vinegar to clean any little insect that may get into the cracks."

"Yes, sir, certainly, sir. Anything I can do to help, sir," she said with another little curtsy.

"Another important thing is what you do with any leftovers from plates, peelings or even things like egg shells. *All* of these things *must* be buried, not left lying around, *not* put in a pile outside and *not* thrown into the river."

"Oh, why not the river, sir?" asked a man I had seen before but never spoken to.

Not knowing what his position was, I assumed he was some sort of butler or the male equivalent of Cook. "I'm sorry, I do not know your name?"

"Oh, it's Peter, sir?" replied the man with a little lowering of the head.

"Well, Peter, the rubbish poisons the river and attracts rats to eat the rubbish. This will poison the people who drink the water downstream."

There was silence and then Edmund noticed that Cook's body language meant she wanted to say something. "Yes, Cook?"

"Begging your pardon, sir, but why should we worry about people downstream?"

This seemed to be a strange question, especially when considering these people were all obsessed with calling themselves Christians. I thought for a couple of seconds and then decided to explain the blindingly obvious. "Cook, if we look after the people downstream, then we can expect the people upstream to do the same for us. We must make sure all the towns and villages are persuaded not to dump their rubbish in the river either."

There was general sighing and shuffling at the enormity of this task. I could imagine them thinking that surely the river was always the natural place for everyone to dump their rubbish. It seemed as if this was going to be a big stumbling block to my ideas, but then Scabbard raised his hand. "Excuse me, sir. I will send messages with the authority of Lord Burford to all settlements upstream. In fact, I shall go there myself tonight!" he exclaimed triumphantly.

"Good man, Scabbard," I responded as I was taken aback by my own presumptuous attitude of superiority, but then I realising that this was what was expected of me and what was necessary if I was to get my point across. I was also beginning to realise that Scabbard was more than just a servant. He was a very capable man who did what he assumed his lord wanted without having to be told each minor detail. I decided that in future I must confide in and trust Scabbard more. He could be nearly as good an ally as Henry Burford and Scabbard had the authority of Henry's father.

At being referred to as a 'good man', Scabbard gave a little nod and seemed to be striving not to show too much pride at this flattery. I wondered if Scabbard's pride was just because it would please his lord or if he genuinely took pride in his own abilities. I was getting a little tired of all the obsequious behaviour and genuflection! I remembered being embarrassed when I accompanied my Catholic friend, Gerry, to his church and saw him genuflecting as he entered the church, and that was in the 21st C.. It seemed like something from a bygone age: *Medieval*! Even in the Middle Ages I found it so degrading for any human being to feel the need to behave like that. Scabbard then went on to say, "I shall arrange for empty corn barrels and pots to be set up outside the kitchen to put things in before we bury them."

"Well done, Scabbard, good idea! It will be possible for some things to be burnt, so only the food waste and similar things need to be buried. Could you arrange that, Scabbard?"

"Thank you, sir, that will be easier. And, yes, I will arrange for the waste to be burnt; or at least that which we cannot feed to the pigs," said Scabbard with another smile of pride and his posture seemed to be more upright than before. *Pigs!* Of course. I hadn't thought of pigs but it was logical that any waste would be fed to the pigs in an agricultural society. Oh well, just another of my period error.

Silence fell and I looked around the kitchen once more. I then turned to Cook and said, "So, I shall leave it up to you, Cook, and I'm sure you will ensure that anything that may attract rats will be removed."

"Oh yes, sir, you can rely on me, sir," she said, beaming with pride yet again.

Turning to Peter, I said, "And I'm sure you will ensure the rest of the house is kept rat free."

"Oh yes, sir, I certainly will and I'll make sure all the house staff know what needs to be done," he said, grinning and nodding.

Then his demeanour changed and he said, "If you wouldn't mind my being so bold, sir, may I offer to get together a group of the young men in the town and organise rat hunts all over the town?"

"Wonderful thinking, Peter; that will be very helpful!"

Peter looked as if all his Christmases had come at once.

"But rats breed so fast we couldn't possibly kill all of them, so what we need to do in the long term is to ensure there is nothing for the next generation of rats to eat. In doing so, they will either go elsewhere or starve to death. However, any rats we can kill now, will help this summer and that is why I want all cats and dogs to be brought into the town to help kill the rats."

The assembled staff received this in polite silence, so I seized the opportunity to take this idea onwards. "Yes, the church is concerned that cats are the work of the Devil, but if we can use cats for God's work, then the Devil will be beaten."

Having said this almost spontaneously, as a paraphrase of what Lord Burford had said to the priest, I was unprepared for what followed. A whoop of joy erupted from all those gathered in the kitchen. Of course, these people believed in the reality of the Devil as much as they believed in the reality of God! Now I felt like Henry V rallying his soldier before Agincourt. However, there was no point in telling the people assembled in the kitchen who Henry V would be!

At this point, I noticed Megan was gesticulating that she had something to say, so I looked at her and enquired, "Yes, Megan, what do you wish to say?"

"Well, sir, as you know, the lord has requested me to help you and Sir Henry around the town in *any* way you want me to."

If you know that I know, then why tell me? It was obvious that she was proud of having been asked this and wanted to advertise it to the rest of the staff rather than inform me. After all, being a Welsh surf probably made her the lowest on the kitchen social scale and this gave her some kudos, so I played the game by saying, "Thank you very much for that, Megan. Sir Henry and I appreciate your vital contribution to the task in hand."

Megan looked like a five-year-old having 'Happy Birthday' sung to her and I was pleased I had made her day – if not her year!

When I was pretty sure that my work in the kitchen was done, I said, "We must move on now, but between keeping the house and kitchen free of food for rats to eat (*I was always careful to avoid the word 'clean' for fear of implying it was not clean now*), Peter's rat hunting parties and Megan helping Sir Henry and I, I'm sure we will do much to diminish the pestilence."

At this, I turned to leave the kitchen, followed by Henry and Scabbard, but as

I did, that little gremlin appeared on my shoulder once more and I could not resist looking at Peter and asking, "You don't know anyone who can play the pipe, do you, Peter?" I wiggled my fingers in front of my mouth to make it clear what I meant.

Peter looked a little confused and said, "Yes, I do, sir. Many people, but why, sir?"

"Oh, never mind," I responded.

As I walked out of the kitchen I heard Henry saying behind me, "Don't let it trouble you, Peter. Sir, de Covny has often said strange things to me that I cannot understand!"

17

The Abbey

Now it was time for the most dangerous part of the 'adventure' so far! It was on to the abbey to see the sick nuns.

Megan had been commissioned to help with 'womanly duties' and the four of us walked out of the house, down the road, across the bridge and into the town: Henry and I in front, followed by Scabbard and then Megan bringing up the rear – in her 'rightful' position. We turned right towards the abbey, at which point I stopped and turned to Henry, Scabbard and Megan.

"Ah hem! This will be an unhealthy place to enter, so there is no need to take unnecessary risks. Why don't the three of you stay outside?"

I was then buried in a torrent of defiant rejection of the idea. Both Henry and Scabbard insisted they must accompany me into the abbey. There seemed to be a number of reasons for this: The nuns had to take the risk, so why shouldn't they? And the 'common people' needed to be set an example and if I would have to enter, then they would accompany me. Megan just remained silent but shook her head when Henry asked if she wished to stay outside. *This is all very honourable*, I thought, *but we need to agree to set certain limits.*

"Okay, but neither Henry, Megan or Scabbard," I said, pointing at each one of them, "should come no further into the room than the door and you are all to avoid touching anything as little as possible in the abbey before washing your hands and bare arms, and again on leaving and when you are back at Burford Hall. Then *all* of you must have a bath and have your clothes washed."

They all agreed! Although this was justified by the risk of infection, I was also calculating that I could have a bath for the first time since I had arrived and have my clothes washed.

As we approached the abbey door, I became aware that there were people gathering around to see them going into the abbey. Was this because of the presence of Henry Burford or the fact that these idiotic people were going into that house of death? Or was it because of this strange young man who had come amongst them with his funny ideas? Perhaps it was a mixture of all three and much else to provide some entertainment before the era of television and 24 hour news.

Before we reached the door, it was opened by the abbess saying, "Welcome, My Lord, sirs and Megan."

"Good day, Reverend Mother," chorused the four of us.

I was clearly settling in with what was expected socially.

"All is ready. Is there anything I can do, sirs?" she added.

Both Henry and Scabbard looked at me. Megan just stood there demurely.

"Yes, Mother," I said, hoping this was the correct form of address. "Please take one large bowl of hot water into the sick room and arrange for four smaller ones to be waiting for us when we depart. All are to have soap with them."

"Yes, sir," replied the abbess with her hands clasped in praying mode.

I then looked at Scabbard and said, "Please hand over those muslin face masks I asked Cook to have prepared."

Scabbard reached into his large bag and got out four strips of muslin that was woven over, time and time again, in the manner I had directed. They were not perfect masks of surgical theatre standard, but it would probably keep out a few germs. They had been tapered at the ends and I placed it over my mouth and nose and tied it behind my head. I then told the three of them to do the same. Although my voice was muffled through the muslin, they clearly understood and did the same.

The abbess politely ignored the strange image these people now presented and led us into the house through a maze of corridors towards the sick room. As agreed, Henry, Scabbard and Megan waited at the door, but I could hardly get into the room as it was full of so many nuns, most of whom appeared to be doing nothing at all except praying on their knees. I was horrified and in a loud voice exclaimed,

"Everyone must leave the room except for *two* – only two – nuns with very good nursing skills."

There was a stunned silence and then a big kerfuffle as the room was emptied except for two nuns; one aged and one quite young.

As the room cleared, I could see that the two nuns were on two beds, in the sheets and covers and as far as I could tell, almost fully clothed. The stench was overwhelming and I was glad I had on the makeshift mask, even if its only purpose was to filter the stink. My eyes quickly scanned the room in the half light, as the curtains were also closed, and settled on a strange pile at the bottom of the two beds. I could not quite see what the pile was made up of, but in a fraction of a second that seemed like minutes, I could see there were lots of different bundles in the pile that all appeared to be roughly the same size. Eventually my eyes focussed in and out as I slowly approached the pile, realising what I was seeing, but then immediately dismissing what my eyes told me. I focussed again, having to admit to myself that my eyes were not deceiving me. It was a pile of *dead pigeons*!

Taking a big step back and trying to hold my breath, I loudly demanded, "Someone, remove all of these dead birds!"

The abbess, who was at the door, started to protest, "But, sir, they are there to help the recovery of the sisters."

"Remove them all immediately and clean the spot where they have been with very hot water and vinegar and then start to clean the rest of the room with *fresh* hot water; everywhere and everything!"

There was a stunned silence and Henry turned to the abbess and gave a gentle nod. The abbess looked at the two remaining nuns and the younger one left the room, presumably to get the hot water and vinegar. Once more I was reminded that without the authority of Lord Burford, through his son, Henry, my words would have no effect at all.

I walked around towards the covered windows. These weren't curtains as I would know them, but merely cloth draped over a hole in the wall with a wooden shutter.

"Please take down these cloths and open the shutters."

There was another gasp from those in the doorway, but this time the other nun immediately started doing as I had bid. Outside it was a warm but breezy day and immediately there was a blaze of light, soon followed by a rush of cool, fresh air. Straight away the atmosphere seemed much more healthy and the two sick nuns sighed as if a great weight had been lifted from them.

"And keep them open, except when it's raining hard or cold at night. Keep the door open as well to create a draught through the room," I said, turning towards the door only to realise that those who had been sent out, where still there, just outside the door and still all mumbling prayers.

"Look, oh dear, everybody except for the abbess, please leave the area. The rest of you can get on with your usual duties. Go to the chapel if you feel the need to pray," I said in an exasperated and what I realised was a rather contemptuous tone, so I added sweetly, "God, will listen to you there."

There was a shuffling in the corridor and the abbess said, "They are asking Our Lady for intercession."

I had no idea who their Lady was, but nodded approvingly. I then stood still for a while trying to compose myself and get my head around the enormity of what I had found. It was no wonder people didn't recover and the disease spread so quickly. Perfectly healthy people would die in circumstances like these. What on earth were the dead pigeons there for? What were they meant to do? Why fill the room with so many people when they knew there was a fatal disease in the room? I told myself it was probably because they believed that being nuns, and praying all the time, God would protect them. It was probably also because they felt the need to suffer and take risks. It was a bit like wearing a hair shirt or those painful garters Opus Dei members wear.

Henry, Scabbard and Megan had remained silent throughout my outburst, but as if Henry could read my mind, he said gently to me, "The sisters had the shutters locked to keep out the miasma." It seemed Henry had been greatly intrigued by his new, curious friend and had tried to get into my head.

Miasma? What was this? Not wanting to show my ignorance, I thought back to my lessons on medieval history and had a vague recollections of a concept that disease was transmitted through the air in a medium they called a miasma.

Realising that my mouth was open, I regained my air of gently didacticism and told Henry, in a loud voice so that the abbess could hear, "The pestilence, or any disease, is not transmitted through a miasma. It is caught by touching the sick, or touching things the sick have touched, or breathing in the breath of the sick. This breath must be cleared from the room by clean, fresh air from the outside. It is not a matter of keeping the 'miasma' out, but getting fresh air in to get the bad air out of the room."

Both Henry and Scabbard nodded whilst Megan gave a serene smile as I looked at the abbess to see her expression of disbelief slowly morph into resigned acceptance of what she must ensure happens.

Henry looked at Scabbard and asked him to get a couple of the makeshift masks for the two nursing nuns. To my surprise, Scabbard opened the large bag he had been carrying and took out two masks. Once more I found myself in a difficult position as I could see Scabbard holding the masks in his hands that may look clean, but were not germ free, and that was a concept I had no time to explain. As Scabbard held up the masks, I turned to the abbess and said, "Reverend Mother, please get another nun to take these masks and wash them in *very* hot water. Dry them outside and then give them to the two nursing nuns. When they have been washed, they must not be touched by anyone who has not *just* washed their hands. And, Scabbard, please get a couple more for them to use when the other masks are being washed at least twice per day." Scabbard reached into his bag again and extracted two more masks.

Now for another difficult order. I walked towards the door to speak directly to the abbess. "Before the two nuns put on their masks, they must wash their whole bodies in as hot water as they can take, and wash their habits as well. Then, when they have put on new habits, find some sort of cloak to cover their whole habits. These cloaks can then be changed and washed twice per day. The nursing sisters *must* wash their hands *every* time they touch the sick patients."

The abbess gave a bemused smile and beckoned down the corridor to convey the orders.

At last there was an opportunity to do what I had come for: Examine the two sick nuns. Walking towards the stiller and quieter of the two patients, I gently rolled back the blanket to reveal a still largely dressed woman, dripping with sweat and who was very smelly. In fact, the stench was overwhelming. I raised her arm and she winced with pain. I could see the large buboes in her armpit and they were oozing with puss. Leaning over the bed and trying not to touch her with my clothing, I pulled her other arm up, causing her more pain, to reveal more oozing buboes. Obviously the nun's groin would also have buboes, but I didn't think it would be acceptable for me to look with Henry, Scabbard and the abbess watching. Anyway, what was the point in looking for the obvious? Her whole body seemed to be covered in boils. Then I saw them. *Leeches!* Lots of them. I took a deep breath – and wished I hadn't. I had no time or patience for diplomacy, so I blurted out, "Get *all* these leeches off her and never put another one on her or *anyone!*"

There was a general hubbub and the abbess began, "But, sir..."

"I don't care, just get them all off and never put any more on her."

There was a further hubbub and I tried to calm myself as I noticed lots of cuts on her veins. It was presumably to bleed what little blood the leeches had left behind. This would be enough to kill even a healthy person, let alone someone suffering from a deadly disease. Gently I turned to those at the door and said, "It is an illusion that she has too much blood or bad blood. She needs every drop of blood to help her recover."

More hubbub followed and the abbess said, "Yes, sir, I do understand and will ensure your commandments are carried out."

I then added, "So no more cutting to bleed her either."

"Yes, sir, I understand," she meekly concurred.

I pulled up the bed clothes and turned to the other sick nun. She seemed to be more restless but this was probably because she was not as ill. As I pulled down the blankets and lifted her arm, she had the strength to assist me, showing that she was the less ill of the two. Of course there were buboes there, but they were not as big as the other sister's and not oozing as much puss. I pulled up the blankets and turned around.

At this point, the nun who had gone to get the hot water and vinegar returned and I spoke to both of the nuns explaining in some detail how they must bathe the two patients' whole bodies in hot water and vinegar. As for the buboes, they must be bathed last and the puss must be removed with a clean cloth before they too are bathed. Then the cloth must be *burnt* – not washed, but burnt. And any time the nursing nuns leave the room, they must wash their hands and anything else that may have touched the sick sisters. Also, the bed clothes must be changed at least once a day and be burnt. *Anyone* who comes in contact with any of these bedclothes must wash as well. The sick sisters must be bathed frequently in warm water, but when they become very fevered, they can be bathed in cold water. They should always try to keep the bed as dry as possible. I had to repeat a few things to ensure I got the point over but I think I made my expectations clear.

"Now, Reverend Mother, that hot water I ordered for us, please?"

As we left I told Scabbard, Henry and Megan to touch nothing on the way out until they had washed. I thought of speaking to the two sick sisters but knew there was little point in their fevered state. Instead I looked at the two nursing nuns saying,

"Thank you for all you are doing."

The two sisters nodded but looked a little shocked that they should be thanked for doing their Christian duty *and* that they should be thanked by someone of such an obviously superior rank. Probably only the Bishop of Gloucester was of a higher rank than someone with the authority of Lord Burford.

As we all left the room, the abbess led the way to the entrance hall where four bowls of steaming water awaited. Henry put his hands behind his head to undo the strings of the mask but I quickly said, "No, wait a minute."

Looking at the abbess, I asked for a cloth to wrap the masks in. The abbess turned to another nun and just looked at her. She disappeared. However, 30 seconds later she reappeared with a cloth. I started to undo my mask signalling to Henry and Scabbard to do the same. All of the masks were laid on the cloth and the three started to wash their hands, faces and any other part of their bodies that had been exposed. Then I pointed to the cloth and the three masks asking the abbess to ensure they were washed, as directed, but only by the two nursing nuns so that no one else came in contact with them.

Suddenly the thought entered my head that I did not know the name of one of the two sick nuns, so I enquired of the abbess, "I know one of the sick sisters is called Sister Cecelia, but what is the name of the other one, please?"

"She is Sister Florence, sir."

"Thank you, and what are the two nursing sisters called?"

"They are both called Sister Magdalene, sir."

"Oh, thank you, Mother Superior," I said with a nod and then wondered if this was how a 'sir' should behave towards an abbess.

Feeling we had done all that was possible, we bid farewell to the nuns and the abbess who assured me that she and the other nuns would continue praying for the recovery of the two sisters, adding rather ominously that if they did not recover, they would pray for their souls. I just could not resist saying, "Oh yes, that will be very helpful."

The abbess, however, took me at face value and looked pleased that this vital contribution was being appreciated.

Outside the abbey a large crowd was waiting for us to emerge. As we did, Scabbard and Megan diverted from Henry and approached a man I did not know. At the same time, Henry said to me, "Are we going to other parts of the town now?"

"Well, I've had a rethink and I think we must now go back to Burford House to wash and change as we have instructed others to do."

"We will do that and I will give you some clothes to change into as you have lost all yours," Henry offered kindly.

"Thank you, Henry." I was relieved at this as I had not changed since I had arrived, having expected to spend only a few hours on my 'travels'. Also, I would fit in better with the 14th century scene, particularly as I assumed they would be clothes of a high-ranking Norman aristocrat. Then Scabbard caught up and told us he had sent Megan off to set another two woman to work on making more masks, and that he had ordered a few other things, such as two men to be in charge of setting up a permanent fire for any of the contaminated items. Once more Scabbard was showing his use and Megan was beginning to play her part too.

Now it was back to Burford House where we could wash and change. As we walked, I casually mentioned to

Henry that is was a strange coincidence that both the nursing sisters were call Magdalene.

"It's not coincidence," answered Henry in a tone that showed his surprise at such a naïve comment.

"No? Why not?" I responded in all innocence

Henry looked uncomfortable and explained quite frankly that this was because they both used to be whores of some sort.

"*Whores*?" I exclaimed.

"Yes, whores. Why else would they be called Magdalene?"

I looked at him open mouthed and he proceeded. "If not actual whores, then loose women or young girls who liked boys too much. They probably got pregnant and that's how they ended up in the abbey."

I looked at Henry again and he added, "You know, whores like Mary *Magdalene*?"

The enormity of what he was saying began to sink in and I remembered the Catholic Church used to take pregnant girls – or those who had given birth or maybe even just had boyfriends and could possibly not be virgins any more – and locked them away in slave camps called laundries to punish them and 'cure' their sexual desires. In Ireland, this had carried on until the very end of the 20th century.

I cogitated and then observed, "So part of the reason they are called Magdalene is so that the world knows about their past?"

"Of course," responded Henry as if I had stated the blindingly obvious.

"And the reason why it is their job to nurse the two sisters is because their lives are worth less than the other sisters?" I asked rhetorically.

"Well, yes, but also because it gives them the chance to cleanse their souls and enter Heaven having spent less time in Purgatory."

"Oh, of course!" I added sarcastically, but Henry didn't catch on.

At this point, we entered Burford House and the conversation ended as we went our separate ways. I had just had a hard reminder that the 14th century was not just like the 21st century but without electricity.

18

It's Later Than You Think

We went back into the house and the usual greeting party was nowhere to be seen. It seemed the fear of where we had been was overpowering. Scabbard said, "I will organise hot baths for you both *immediately*, sirs."

I looked at Scabbard and knew I had to make sure he would not contaminate anything, or anyone, including us, by not cleaning himself first.

"Scabbard, I know you like to serve us but..."

"It is my duty, sir," interjected Scabbard with a very indignant tone in his voice.

I took a deep breath and chose my words carefully. "Yes, Scabbard, but in order to serve us, you must remain fit and well. You will be no good to me, Sir Henry or the lord if you are ill or even dead."

I paused for a while and allowed Scabbard to absorb this. "So, before you get our baths ready, I want you to take your clothes off and soak them in hot water, without anyone else touching them, and then have a hot bath yourself before preparing our baths."

Scabbard looked confused and looked at Henry who gave him a slight smile. Scabbard then looked at me and said, "As you wish, sir."

Scabbard turned to leave and I added, "Oh, and give the same instructions to Megan."

"Yes, sir," he replied with a half-turn and then disappeared leaving Henry and I to go to our respective rooms and wait.

I sat on my bed with a mix of emotions. It varied between being rather fearful of what I may have caught and boredom because of waiting for the bath. There was no TV to watch, no internet to play with, no Ipod to listen to, and not even a book to read. They had books in the middle of the 14th century, but Chaucer was a little young to be prolific yet and, anyway, I had read most of his stuff. Thinking of this, I began to think that without this love of Chaucer, I may not be here. Or if I was, I would not understand people and would have no chance of making myself understood. Was this just luck or had some force brought me here for a reason? If so, why? The time lords would not have allowed me to do all the things I was doing if it would alter the future. The philosophical debate about a man who goes back and kills his own grandfather, which he could not do because that would mean he would never be born in order to go back and do it, kept running through my head. No matter how much I rationalised things, I could not avoid thinking that this was all part of a plan. How else could it have happened? But whose plan and why should I be chosen to carry it out? Perhaps there is a God. If so, surely he had more effective ways of helping people through the Black Death? After all, he is omnipotent – allegedly! The time lords would not have approved, so who did? Or what? And why? Perhaps it was the fairies. That seems as reasonable as it being the time lords or God!

Suddenly I felt tired, probably because of the stress, and I lay on my bed for a rest. That was the last I remembered until I became aware of loud knocking on my door.

"Who? What? Where am I? Oh, er, come in!"

"Sorry to wake you, sir," said Scabbard, standing in the doorway. "Your bath is waiting, sir."

"Em, yes, I'm coming. I didn't mean to fall asleep." I followed Scabbard to a room where a tub with almost boiling water was waiting.

"There you are, sir, and there are some of Sir Henry's clothes for you to change into."

"Thank you, Scabbard," I said as the door closed behind him.

Cautiously dipping my toe into the hot water I realised it was hotter than I would get into at home. Having said that it should be as hot as possible, I could hardly complain and there was no cold tap. One foot was lowered in and the water came halfway up my calf. It was just about bearable but I pulled it out again and looked at the red mark. I put it back in and it was less painful this time. Now the other leg went in and I was standing in the tub. Slowly I lowered my bottom until it touched the water. "Aah!" I yelled and got out again. It took me at least five minutes to sit down and then I looked around for some soap. There it was on a small table next to the bath tub. The tub itself appeared to be made of wooden planks and held together with metal stave – rather as an old beer barrel would have been. It gentle oozed water. Well, I found what I supposed was meant to be soap, although, what it was made of, I didn't like to think about. It was probably some sort of tallow. Having washed my body I wondered what to do with my hair. I had no choice other than to use the 'soap'. By now the water was cool enough to put my head under, though there was not a lot of room to move in the tub. If this was what the very rich had to bathe in, what did the poor use? They probably had nothing at all. Once I had wet my hair, I began to work the soap into it. Then there was a knock at the door.

"Come in."

The door opened and Scabbard stood there with a sort of sheet in his hands.

"I've come to get your clothes to wash it, sir."

"Oh, yes, thank you, Scabbard."

He came and picked up the clothes in the sheet, being careful not to touch them. He had clearly taken on board my instructions and this time I couldn't help but notice how clean Scabbard looked. He walked towards the door with his bundle and turned to say, "Thank you, sir."

I gave a little nod, slowly learning that I had probably been treating Scabbard with more respect than our respective class positions would dictate. Scabbard went out again, leaving me to finish off washing my hair and then lie in the bath and soak for a while – the most luxurious feeling I had had since I arrived.

After a long while, the too hot bath began to get a little cool, so I stood up and looked at my lobster-like body. No permanent harm was done, though. It was just a very hot bath. Sorting through the clothes Scabbard had left behind, it was difficult to work out what went on first and where. Suddenly I realised that Scabbard would be a little confused when he sees my underpants. *Oh, sod it,* I thought. It was too late now anyway and they can't be more confusing than many other things about a man from the 21st C.. In the pile of clothes I found an undershirt, a tunic, a sleeveless jacket, long socks (or stockings) and, to my surprise, a pair of basic briefs. Donning them all I felt a bit like a pantomime character and, also, more comfortable to know that I would fit in better in the 14th century.

I stepped out and into the reception area, which was empty, and now I had no idea what to do as this was the first time I had been alone, except in my bedroom. Hopping from foot to foot for a while, I decided to wander around the house. No sooner had I taken a few steps than one of the kitchen staff came out of a door and stopped, staring at me.

"Hello. Oh, uhm, good day."

Her eyes moved up and down and after apparently realising that I was wearing different clothes, her expression of apprehension turned to a smile. "Oh, there will be some food served soon, sir."

"Oh, thank you, I'll be upstairs."

Back in my room, I was once more filled with the sense of a lack of entertainment. It was difficult to cope without the 21st century's distractions. How would Henry cope in the 21st century? We will never know! Looking out of the window and across the estate, I could see a bath being filled outside. What was going on? Was someone else having a bath? Looking out towards Swinbrook, I could see the small village which only consisted of a few houses, but I couldn't help but think that it had not grown much over the next nearly 700 years. As I looked around and time passed, a number of buckets of hot water were brought out to the bath and then a naked man emerged from the house and dipped his toe into the bath just as I had done earlier. As I watched, feeling a bit like a pervert, there was a knock at the door.

"Come in."

"Sir, are you ready for dinner?" asked Scabbard as he opened the door.

"Oh, yes. I'll come down now."

Scabbard waited at the open door and I followed him down to the dining room where he held the door open for me.

Henry was already sitting at the table and I walked in to Henry's greeting of, "Come in. Sit down." He gestured with his hand to the place opposite him.

As I sat down, I noticed four places were set. Henry and I now began to chat like two old friends who are very close when the door opened and in walked the lord and lady. Standing up I gave a slight bow and sat again as they took their seats. Clearly the lord wanted a report on the morning's proceedings, so we both started recounting. The table was still bare of food and as Henry and I were recounting the day's events, the door opened again and in walked Megan with a large tray. I was seated opposite the door and glanced up and then turned towards Lord Burford again, only to look back at Megan as my jaw dropped at the vision of loveliness that had just walked through the door. For the first time, I saw her with her hair clean and brushed. Previously I had thought I would fancy her if she was cleaned up, but I never thought she'd be this gorgeous. Being slim and young she looked good without a bra, but I had previously noticed how older, bigger women looked saggy and shapeless without a bra. I became aware that I was staring, so I closed my mouth and forced myself to look away. Megan put the food down as she shyly caught my eye. Previously she had not flirted in Lord Burford's presence, but she must have realised I was staring and could not resist responding. Having placed the food on the table she walked towards the door and gave a quick look back as she exited, just to make sure I was still looking. I was.

Struggling to get my mind off the lovely Megan, I joined Henry in telling about our visit to the abbey. As Henry had not been shocked by what we found and it was no more than he had expected, he left it largely to me to tell about the horrors of the dead pigeons, blood letting, closed windows and leaches. Lord Burford took a deep interest in the 'funny' ideas I had and seemed to be convinced by my argument that blood was necessary for good health and reducing it was not a good idea at all. As for the dead pigeons, he didn't appear to be at all convinced as to the efficacy of this 'treatment' anyway. What was more difficult to get over, was the concept that there was no such thing as a miasma.

"Surely there must be," said the lord, "or else how did disease get transmitted from one sick person to another?"

Not feeling able to go into detail about oxygen, nitrogen and carbon dioxide, I restricted myself to saying that little animals inside the sick person were coughed or sneezed out and then went onto other people. "Yes, we can see little drops flying around when people cough," the lord added helpfully.

"Ah, but that is not only liquid. The tiny animals are inside the droplets," I replied, restraining myself from talking about how viruses cause the body to cough or sneeze, just so that they can spread themselves to other hosts.

The idea of a tiny animal that could think for itself would just be too much for a medieval man, even if he clearly did have an intelligent mind. Anyway, I was obviously winning over the most powerful man in town, so there was no need to over complicate the issue. At this point, I remembered an expression my father used ever since I could remember. It was, 'coughs and sneezes spread diseases'.

Lord and Lady Burford liked this, as did Henry, so I latched onto it and repeated it many times. There was a pause and I could not resist asking, "Is this chicken?"

"No, it is goose!" said Lady Burford, surprised that I did not know the difference, but I had never eaten goose.

"But what can we do," asked the lord, wanting to get to the cure rather than the theory.

"Well, we must impress on *everybody* not to sneeze on anyone else and to blow their noses on rags. Those who do have kerchiefs, must wash them very often and replace it with new ones as often as possible. This really is vital if we are to stop the spread of this pestilence or any other disease." I toyed with the idea of asking him to stop people constantly spitting in the street, but refrained from doing so, as I felt this would probably be asking too much. He may simply ask where else they should spit and I'd have no answer.

"Mmm," replied the lord. He picked up a small bell on the table and shook it. Within seconds Megan appeared at the door. She must have been waiting outside. She entered, curtsied and asked, "My Lord?"

"Oh Megan, ask Scabbard to come here, would you?"

"Yes, My Lord." She curtsied again and left the room.

At this point, I couldn't help but note how relatively polite Lord Burford was to a person of such a low social order. She was not just a maid but also probably not free, either a surf or a villain, and even worse, she was *Welsh!*

Soon Scabbard appeared and the lord indicated for him to pull up a chair near to the table; not actually at the table.

"Edmund, would you repeat to Scabbard your explanation about coughs and sneezes."

"Yes, sir," I obliged and off I went repeating what I had said before, but this time a little more succinctly. I also got Scabbard to repeat "Coughs and sneezes spread diseases! Coughs and sneezes spread diseases! Cough and sneezes spread diseases!"

Then Lord Burford added, "Now makes sure everybody in the town knows this."

"Yes, sir," Scabbard said as he departed.

I was impressed that before the 21st century's age of mass media it was still possible to spread health education.

The conversation moved on and Lord Burford ask the awkward question I was fearing. "Will the sisters survive?"

I took a deep breath and said, "To be honest, I don't know, but their chances will be increased if the abbey follows my instructions. More importantly, it will increase the chances of other people *not* getting the disease which is far more helpful."

"Mmm, yes. I have issued instructions that if anyone else is afflicted, they are to be kept in their homes by boarding them up along with their family."

I was shocked to *silence*! Then I chose my words carefully and, as respectfully as I could, offered some advice. "May I suggest that only the sick person is boarded into his or her home but that the rest of the family is moved elsewhere and kept separate from the rest of the town's folk?"

There was another silence – a thoughtful one – as Lord Burford decided whether or not this was a good idea or even possible. After few seconds, the lord looked at me so I added, "If we board the whole family into the house, inevitably almost all will get the disease, but if we isolate the other family members, they are likely to survive but won't infect others."

"Mmm, all right. When Scabbard returns I will tell him to arrange for one of the barns to be used for these people."

Barn, I thought, but kept quiet. After all, it was summer and the alternative was much worse. I allowed myself a warm feeling.

At this point, there was a knock on the door and Megan entered with another little curtsy and I wondered how old people behaved when their knees were too stiff to do regular curtsying.

"Sir, Father McKenzie is here and wishes to speak to you, sir."

"Oh, send him in, Megan."

She disappeared and with a raised eyebrow Lord Burford asked rhetorically, "I wonder what he wants."

Father McKenzie entered and with his hands together in prayer mode gave an obsequious smile and bow, saying, "My Lord, My Lady, Sir Henry, Sir Edmund."

Sir, eh? I thought to myself. *At least he knows his place!*

"Yes, Father, what do you want?" asked Lord Burford rather curtly.

"Sir, I have heard of the good work being done today in the abbey." He paused.

"Yes?" Lord Burford encouraged him to go on.

"So I would like to say a special mass in the church tonight to ask the Lord our God to give his blessing to the work being done in the temporal world."

"Oh, yes, Father. What time do you suggest?"

"It's entirely up to you, sir," Father McKenzie replied, becoming even more obsequious.

"Shall we say the eighth hour, Father?"

"Yes, that would be perfect, sir," the priest replied as he shuffled backwards and out of the door, bowing so low that I wondered if he was in a yoga class.

As the door closed, Lord Burford lowered his head and issued the soliloquy. "And a good donation from me for *another* special mass, no doubt!"

I understood I had a greater ally in Lord Burford than I had realised. There was no doubt that he believed there was a family of Gods in the sky pulling the strings, but he seemed aware of the self-serving nature of the church.

The eighth hour, I thought to myself and glanced out of the window to see the lengthening shadows and realised it was a lot later than I had thought. How long did I sleep for after returning from the abbey? The idea that Henry and I would go around town this afternoon would now obviously have to be left until tomorrow. At this point, there was a knock at the door and Megan entered again with another tray of food and put a bowl in front of me. As I began to eat, it appeared to be some sort of pudding made with flour, honey and plums.

"Ah, fruit," I said, more to myself than anyone else.

"You like fruit, do you, Edmund?" asked Lady Burford.

"Yes, I do and this is really delicious," I replied quite genuinely.

"Good," Lady Burford said with a flow of pride.

Even though she had probably not cooked it, she obviously felt she was being complimented. As we were finishing our meals, I looked at the lord and enquired, "Did I, erm, see a bath being prepared in the garden earlier on?"

"Yes, we thought as Megan and Scabbard were bathing, the rest of the staff may as well do so as well. After all, it is such a lovely summer's day." I hoped that this idea might catch on!

Soon the meal was over and all departed the dining room. Henry and I walked together and I asked, "Do you have anything I could read please, Henry?"

"Yes, of course," said Henry turning in his stride and going back the other way. Coming to a door, Henry opened it to reveal a library full of books. I beamed and started to look along the shelves.

"I'll leave you to it," said Henry, disappearing.

I looked at the hundreds of books all made of materials other than paper. There were hundreds of titles and names I had never heard of, even though I had spent years studying medieval literature. Finally a title caught my eye. *The Divine Comedy* by Dante Alighieri. This was a book I had heard of but never read. Plucking it off the shelf, I hurried to my room to read this gem of poetic literature. Once I was in my room, I flung myself on my bed and began to read. What would my English teacher, Miss Stables, think of this? Not only was I reading the famous *Divine Comedy*, but I was reading it in its original medieval English language in a genuine medieval book. So entranced was I that I did not notice the passage of time and felt deprived when Henry knocked on my door and walked in.

"Time to go, Edmund."

The two of us walked to the main door of the house and Henry asked, "Are you enjoying the book?" "Yes, I am." That little gremlin once more appeared on my shoulder, so I added, "But I have not yet reached *The National Express* or *The frog princess.*"

"Er, I do not remember those."

"Oh, never mind."

"That was another of your obscure comments, wasn't it?"

I just smiled as we reached the great door where it seemed the whole Burford House was waiting. I felt a little guilty as I was sure the lord and lady should not be kept waiting.

"Sorry to keep you all waiting," I said a little nervously.

"Pay that no mind," said Lord Burford kindly and the others mumbled in respectful agreement.

Off we all went and just before we reached St. John the Baptist's church, the lord came up to me and said quietly, "You will be careful, won't you, Edmund?"

"Yes, sir, of course I will." Lord Burford nodded and we entered the church.

This time the service or ceremony, I was not quite sure what it was, passed relatively quickly as the priest stood at the front, apparently talking to himself and all the others chanted when required. I joined in too as I was getting better at this ritual. Soon it was all over and Father McKenzie hurried to the door to do a bit more grovelling as Lord and Lady Burford passed through the door. By the shadows outside I estimated we had been inside for about half an hour. I did not know how much of a donation Lord Burford would be expected to give, but guessed it would be quite a lot for half an hour's work. *Oh well, what price could be put on God's blessing?* I thought to myself. As we walked away from the church, Father McKenzie watched us. Then he turned to another priest and said, "We must watch that one. I think the Bishop of Gloucester should know."

Back at Burford House, Henry said to me, "Have another read. There will be some supper just before dusk."

At a guess it was now about the ninth hour, so I guessed I had about one hour to read my new found love as it was still virtually midsummer and remained just about light enough till about 10 pm I was engrossed in the book, so when there was a knock on the door, I called out, "Come in."

The door opened to reveal Megan with a bowl and a towel. "This is for you, my good sir, and supper will be ready when you have washed."

"Thank you, Megan."

She put down the bowl and just seemed to hang around. I did not know how to take this and stumbled to say, "Thank you for your help today. It was very useful."

She smiled and gave a nervous little curtsy. I was sure she was doing more than just flirting, but I simply did not know how to get off with a girl from the middle ages, especially as she was nearly 700 years old. Eventually the conversation ground to a halt and Megan edged towards the door and closed it behind her. *Oh my God! Have I blown it?* But if I had made a move, what about later on? It was probably best I didn't.

I quickly washed and went downstairs to the dining room. No one was there yet, but on the table was a sumptuous choice of breads and cheeses, plus, of course, the ubiquitous beer. I had had quite a lot of beer at the previous meal and perhaps that was why the special mass seemed to pass so quickly. Soon Henry walked in and we sat and chatted about the day and nothing at all really. The breads were all a little too heavy for my liking, but the cheese was lovely and very flavoursome. The conversation went on until it was completely dark which I estimated was about half past ten. So Henry and I withdrew to our respective rooms and I slipped my clothes off and fell on the bed. There was no time to think about the day as sleep came almost instantly.

19

Around the Town: Morning

I got up the next morning and went down for breakfast. Having been here – or was it there – for a few days now, I was beginning to experience it all as normal. Rising, washing in the water brought by Scabbard, and having breakfast seemed no surprise and of little consequence. Henry was already waiting and the two of us chatted about the day ahead.

Meeting Scabbard and Megan at the door, we were off towards the abbey. Before we got there, I stopped and turned to the other three. "We will not go into the abbey, but just chat at the door."

"Is that to avoid the pestilence?" asked Henry.

"Yes, partly. There's no point in taking unnecessary risks and, also, we don't need to go through the same procedure as yesterday *unless* there is a problem we need to go in for".

"All right."

Then Megan opened her mouth as if to speak and closed it again.

"Yes, Megan, what do you want to say?" I asked.

"Well, sir, I was just wondering... if..."

"Yes, Megan, get to the point, please."

"Well, sir, I thought it might be good if I went into the abbey to check if everything is being done properly."

I looked at her.

Then she gabbled, "Oh no, sir. Sorry, sir! I didn't mean to be presumptuous, sir. It's just that, well, I think I know what you require, sir, and I thought I could be of more help to you, sir, but I didn't mean to... Oh, er, sorry, sir."

I gathered my thoughts and said, "Yes, Megan, that is a very good thought." There was a long pause. "But you are aware it increases your chances of catching the disease?"

"Yes, sir, but if it will help the nuns..."

"Okay, well I will speak to the reverend mother and explain things. You are only to go in and see what's going on and give instructions. Do not stay longer than is necessary. Is that okay?"

There was another long silence. "Sir, I don't know what the word 'okay' means?"

Henry jumped in by saying, "Yes, I have also been wondering about that, Edmund. You keep on using the word."

Suddenly realising I had used a word that was not used in the 14th century, tried to explain it away. "Oh, er, sorry. It's a word we use at home. It means 'Is everything good?' or 'Are you happy?' It's used to confirm something or as an interrogative."

"Oh, I see," said Henry.

Quickly moving the conversation on, I told Megan, "I want you to come to the door with me and I will tell the reverend mother you are here to oversee my instructions and then you are to leave."

"Okay," replied Megan with a smile and we all approached the abbey door watched by a gathering crowd like yesterday. Before we could get there, however, it was opened by a nun saying, "Come in, sirs."

"No, Sister, we will not *all* come in today, but may I speak to the reverend mother?"

"Yes, sir, she is on her way."

"Thank you."

There then followed a few seconds of nervous waiting as the nun hopped from foot to foot. Then the abbess arrived. "Good day to you all. Please come in."

"No, Mother. I spoke yesterday before about *unnecessary* risks, so we will not all come in, but Megan will go in to see how the sisters are..."

"Oh, they seem more comfortable..." interjected the abbess.

"Good! So, Megan will carry out my wishes and then leave," I said, trying to give an air of authority.

The abbess looked at Megan rather questioningly but said, "Come in, Megan."

Megan bent down, opened her bag, took out her muslin mask and began to put it on. The thought passed through my head that I should check whether it has been washed or whether it was a new one, but I restrained myself realising that Megan was an intelligent girl and she was proving a great asset to me in the situation. I got the impression the abbess was rather put off by the idea of such a young girl being put in charge, but further admired Megan for her courage and maturity. As she entered, I said, "Thank you, Reverend Mother. Megan knows what is required." I was trying to give Megan a bit of back up and then turned to walk away. Henry and Scabbard followed.

As we walked I turned to Henry and asked, "Is the abbess a bit put off that such a young girl should be delegated to giving orders?"

There was a second's pause and Henry said, "I suppose by 'put off' you mean a little insulted?"

"Yes," I replied, realising I had done it again.

"That is one reason, yes, but I think the main reason is because she is only a surf."

I had not thought of this but remembered from the doomsday book that the word 'surf' and 'slave' were used interchangeably. It dawned on me that Megan had no rights whatsoever. She owned nothing and could do nothing, or go nowhere, without permission of the lord of the manor. She may not be in shackles but legally was no more free than a Negro on a sugar plantation. But where would she go anyway? Her parents had been killed in one of the wars in Wales, so she was probably lucky to be alive and have a place to live and food to eat. There were no social services who would have looked after her in Wales, and there probably were hundreds of Welsh children in the same position who simply starved to death. Such were the middle ages!

"Sir Edmund," said Scabbard and I turned to look around, realising Scabbard was hanging back. He probably wanted a talk, rather than the odd word, so I stopped and listened along with Henry.

"I have been around the town and at any house where there is some sort of sickness, someone will meet us and tell us the problem."

"Oh, good. You have done well, Scabbard. That will save us wasting time."

"And, um, the blacksmith humbly requests you go into the forge to discuss something he is doing for the lord."

"Oh, well, yes, we can do that," I replied, wondering what it was all about.

As usual, the town was full of market stalls and business was being conducted. An uncomfortable thought crossed my mind and I turned to Henry and asked, "How do all these products get into the town?"

"They came in through the official points and all care has been taken to check where they came from."

"Good, but I am concerned that the sisters probably got the infection from some of the clothes brought into the town."

"If I may help there, sir?" offered Scabbard.

"Of course, go on, Scabbard."

"We now know that the two sisters visited a sick household in Alvescot and that must have been where they got the sickness from."

"Oh, I see! Well, that's good to know. At least now we understand how it got into the town. But it shows how careful everybody needs to be."

"Yes, sir, but the nuns must visit the sick, if only just to pray for them."

I nodded. What else could I do? The nuns were, knowingly, risking their lives to help these people. I could hardly tell them they should not. They may be of some help and even the prayers may give help and some solace to those who believe – which, of course, *everybody* did in the Middle Ages. Probably the most effective medicine they had was the placebo effect. Anyway, what use were nuns if they did not help the sick and pray for them? Without that belief, there would be no point in being a nun.

We carried on with business and walked up the road where a woman stood in the road and approached Scabbard as we passed. *Why Scabbard?* It's probably because she was too humble to approach the lord's son. This woman was one of those who was to wait outside if they wanted a visit from the strange 'doctor'. Scabbard looked at me and told me that the woman's husband has been ill for few days.

"Well, tell me your husband's symptoms, Madam?" I asked the woman.

"What, sir?"

"What is wrong with your husband?"

"Oh sir, he has been ill for a few days."

"Yes?"

"He is very weak, feverish, often sick and keeps shitting."

"All right, we will come in and see," I said, consciously avoiding the term 'okay'.

All three of us donned our makeshift masks, which caused the woman to look at us quizzically, and followed her into the house. In a chair sat a middle aged man, fully dressed and soaked in what was probably sweat.

"John, John," said the woman. "Sir Henry and Sir Edmund have come to see you."

"No, no, I'm all right, I haven't got the pestilence."

Clearly the poor man was more concerned with the consequences of having the plague than anything else. He didn't want his house to be boarded up with his family inside, all virtually facing certain death.

"It's all right, John," I said reassuringly, "just let me have a look at you." Turning to the woman, I asked, "What's your name, Madam?"

"Oh, it's Maria, sir, and my children are..."

"Yes, yes, Maria. Can you help me take his top clothes off?"

"Oh, certainly, sir."

The two of us struggled to get his top clothes off as John continued to protest his perfect health. When his chest was exposed, I lifted his arm whilst asking Maria,

"How long did you say he had been ill?"

"Oh, two or three days now, sir." This was reassuring, as any symptoms would have become apparent by now if it were the bubonic plague.

Lifting his arm there was a smell of stale sweat, but nothing at all to compare with the stench that surrounded the sick nuns. Mind you, there were no dead pigeons either. Looking into his hairy armpit was not a pleasant experience, so I lowered it as quickly as possible. Then I turned John around to look at the other.

Lowering the second arm, I looked at Maria and said, "I don't know exactly what is wrong with John, but I am as sure as one can be that he does not have the plague." There was a 'whoop' from Maria and a string of names erupted from her as ten years appeared to disappear from the woman's face. In through the door came a stream of children of varying ages all running to their mother and father who fell into what looked like an oversize tubby cuddle.

"Woe, woe, woe!" I exclaimed. "I said he doesn't have the plague, but that doesn't mean he's not infectious."

"Oh, sir?" responded the mother, looking confused.

"D and V can be very contagious, so keep yo..."

"What, sir?"

"Diarrhoea and vomiting."

"Eh?"

"Shit and sickness!"

"Oh, er, sir, but he's not going to die?"

"Probably not, but the children must keep their distance until he starts to get better and you may tend him by washing him frequently with cool water. Try to get him to eat as much as possible. Maybe some soup."

"Soup, sir?" she asked as she looked around nervously at the fire with a pot on it.

"We only have pottage, sir."

I moved to the fire and looked at the blackened pot with some sludge in it.

"What is in this?"

"Oh, root vegetables, peas, oats and anything else we have, sir."

I realised then that this was their main diet, so I said, "Give him some of the liquid until he gets stronger. Then you can give him the thicker bits. And, er, keep the..." I looked around for windows but there were none really, just holes with wood in them. "Keep the, er, door open as much as possible. Take his clothes off and put him to bed till he can stand easily. Then wash his clothes and the bed he's been in."

"Oh, yes, sir, that I can do now. It's the middle of summer."

"Good."

"Are you sure he will not die, sir?"

"Not if you follow my instructions, Maria."

"Oh, I will, sir. Out you go children! Get on with your work and I will bring you some food later. Oh, thank you, sir. Thank you. Thank you. Thank you!"

Henry, Scabbard and I hurried out and I removed my mask, as did the other two.

"I want to wash," I said to no one in particular.

"There is a trough up here, sir," Scabbard offered.

A trough! *Oh dear, where can I start*, I thought to myself. Oh well, it's better than nothing I suppose. When we got to the trough, I said to Scabbard, "Use that little bucket to pour water onto my hands so that the water does not go back into the trough". This Scabbard did for me and then for Henry. Finally, I poured water onto Scabbard's hands who seemed very embarrassed that I should serve him.

On we went, followed by a growing crowd, to a large building that was emitting smoke and a funny smell along with it.

"This is the foundry," said Henry and we turned to go in.

As we entered we were hit by a wall of heat. Men were running around all over the place and sparks were flying. I thought to myself that I had never been big on health and safety, but a few goggle wouldn't go amiss. Work virtually stopped as the foundry workers looked at us and the usual bowing and scraping commenced. A man who appeared to be some sort of foremen approached us and began to talk to Henry. He had an old, lined and rubid face that was probably the result of working next to such heat. I couldn't help but notice that the man's hands and arms were covered in scars, probably caused by sparks from the furnace or drops of hot iron. He looked to be in his 70s or 80s but I wondered how old he really was. I was so intent on working out the man's age that I hardly heard him tell Henry that the reason why I was wanted was in the next section.

Henry, Scabbard and I filed through the foundry and into the next area where there was another furnace. It immediately became obvious that this was not an iron foundry but a glass making factory. Two fires were burning and spitting with large pots boiling with what was obviously glass. Once more work virtually stopped as we entered and, much to my relief, we stopped at the edge of the working area as a man approached us. He too was covered in little scars but did look younger than the other man. More bowing and scraping followed and then Henry said to me, "This is Harold, the chief glass smith and he would like some help on making the right sort of glass for the star looker."

Oh my God, I thought. He thinks I know what I'm talking about! Oh well, better try to blag it like I have with virtually everything else since I've been here. I turned to Harold and asked, "Have you got some examples of glass that has not come out perfectly and has distortions in it?"

"Oh, yes, sir, we've got plenty of those. If you'd like to come outside with us..."

Henry and I nodded and the man walked towards a side door followed by Henry, Scabbard and me.

At the door there was a little bit of confusion as Harold opened the door, went through it, and immediately scurried back to hold the door for his betters as we went through. Once outside, Harold directed us towards a few large boxes all filled with broken glass. Looking in but not wanting to put my hand in, I looked for a good piece of distorted glass and then leant forward to carefully pick it up.

"Oh no, sir, you let me do that, sir," said Harold, quickly going to pick up the piece. Holding it up I lowered myself slightly to look through the distorted bit. Then, getting into my role of a Norman aristocrat, I said, "Could you pick out a few bits like that, my man."

Harold quickly produced 5 or 6 similar bits of broken glass and I said, "You see how, as the light passes through the distorted part, things on the other side look bigger and misshapen?"

"Oh yes, sir, I have noticed that before, sir."

"Well, that's what we want, but without the misshapen bits, so try to make it as good as possible."

Harold looked a bit confused and grunted, so I tried to clarify the point by saying,

"Try to make it convex."

"Eh, sir?"

"Try to make it so it is thicker in the middle than it is at the edges."

"Oh, I see, sir."

"Do you think you can do that, Harold?"

"Oh yes, sir, I can certainly do that, sir. Oh yes, sir, don't you worry about that, sir."

"Good. Then get two bits of tubing, one sligh..."

"Of what, sir?"

"Tubing!" There was no response. "Piping?"

"Oh yes, sir, I can do that, sir."

I thought and then added, "But not made of pottery or terracotta. It needs to be very thin and very light in weight."

Harold looked thoughtful and then smiled and said, "Oh yes, sir. I think I can do that, sir."

"Good. One must fit very tightly inside the other so it slides in and out. Then you put the glass at each end and slide in an out till you get a good focus on the moon."

"The moon?"

Realising my literal interpretation, I said, "For example."

Still there was no reaction.

"Or a star."

"Oh yes, sir. Yes, sir, yes, sir."

"Then you need to just keep trying different sorts of glass and length of tubing... er, piping, till you get a good picture of the moon or whatever."

"Yes, sir, uhm, er, how do I get the glass to stay at the end, sir?"

Realising I could be there all day, I started to move off saying, "I'm sure you can find a way, Harold. I have total faith in *you*, Harold."

"Oh yes, sir. Yes, sir. Oh, er, this way out, Sirs. This way out, sirs," Harold said as he lead us out around the side of the foundry to the road. "It will mean you don't have to go through the heat, sirs."

This pleased me and I was relieved to reach the street again.

Then Henry said to Harold, "Good day, Harold."

Harold clearly understood this meant to clear off now. We started moving up the road and although I was pleased to have avoided the heat, I rather wished I'd taken more notice of how the foundry and glass works operated.

At this point, Scabbard came up close behind us and began to speak to us both. "There is a family here who would like to talk to you, Sir Edmund."

"Yes?"

"Not because they think they have the disease, but the son has a strange sort of, er, er, er, possession."

Scabbard seemed to whisper the word 'possession' as if it were something dirty and unmentionable.

"Oh well, we had better have a look."

"The house is here, sir."

As we turned towards the house, I became aware that there were men in the street shovelling up the piles of horse shit. Wondering what they would do with it, I realised it would be spread on the land around the town as manure. There would certainly be fewer flies. Then my mind turned to the thought that Scabbard always managed to remain a respectful distance behind. What a degrading, feudal culture. Then I remembered that Phil always keeps a respectful distance behind Betty and he's been doing it for decades. *A degrading feudal culture, indeed*!

Before we reached the door, it was opened by a bedraggled little man who was dirtier than most and looked as though he could do with a good meal. Scabbard walked up to us and said, "Sirs, this is Edward and his son, also Edward, is the afflicted one."

"All right, we had better see him."

"Sir, sir," said Edward "He appears well, but sometimes..."

"Yes, Edward, let me see him."

We stepped into the house for which the word 'hovel' seemed to have been coined, and there was a very unpleasant smell. The smell of poverty! There was young Edward sitting on a stool and standing in a dark corner was a woman, presumably the wife and mother.

"Do you think we could move closer to the door way?" I asked. "There I will be able to see better." I needed any excuse to get away from the smell.

"Now, Edward, tell me what is wrong with young Edward?" Looking at the lad, I thought he looked about 10 or 11.

"Well, sir, most of the time Edward if very well and then sometimes he... he... throws himself to the floor and, er, twitches and there is nothing we can do to stop this. Then he wakes up and seems... and seems... normal but he is always very tired and has no memory of what has happened."

"Mmm! Scabbard, may I talk to you?"

"Of course, sir."

I led Scabbard outside, followed by Henry who was equally pleased to leave the smell. "Scabbard, I assume you know the family?"

"Yes, sir, I know all the families in the town."

"And what can you tell me about the boy?"

"What do you want to know, sir?"

"How old is he?"

"14 years old, sir."

"14?"

"Yes, sir."

"They, uhm, seem very poor."

"That is because Edward cannot get much work because young Edward is possessed, sir." The whole family is cursed by young Edward's possession.

"I see. Of course."

"Come back in with me, Scabbard, and listen carefully to what I say as I want you to make sure the whole town knows what I have to say."

Inside, the family looked anxious and Henry, sensibly, stood at the door. The woman was standing by the doorway as I re-entered, so I asked her, "And what is your name?"

"Marie, sir," said the mother with a little curtsy.

I proceeded to try to explain to the family, Henry and, most importantly, Scabbard as he would have to put the word around town.

"Edward suffers from what is known as epilepsy."

Silence filled the room.

"That means he..."

"We have had many special masses said for him, sir," interjected the father.

This gave me a moment to think. There was no point in my explaining about electrical convulsions in the brain. Eventually, I found words I hoped would put the point over.

"You know when people sometimes get cramps in their leg and it is very painful, with no control at all of the leg?"

"Oh yes, sir."

"Well, Edward gets cramps in his brain... in his head, and that means he has no control of his body for a while, just like someone who has no control of their leg for a while."

There was a long silence and then Edward asked, "What can we do about it, sir?"

"Nothing at all, just as there is nothing you can do for someone who has a leg cramp." A sense of despondency descended upon the house.

"But I have no doubt that Edward is *not* possessed by demons or the Devil."

"Not possessed by the Devil, sir?"

"No, Edward. It is probably congenital... in the family. There was probably another person in the family who had the same problem."

Marie 'whooped' and hid her head in her hands. Edward screamed, "You knew, Marie. You knew!"

"Edward, listen to me and listen carefully. It is not Marie's fault! It is not Marie's fault any more than it is Edward's fault. There is no possession going on. We will tell the world and from now on your life, and the life of your family, will get much better. You will be able to hold your head up in the town and all will know you are good people." There was a slow realisation as the parents and the child began to understand. As I walked towards the door, I said to Scabbard, "You know what to do, don't you?"

"I think I do, sir. Yes, sir."

I knew Scabbard well enough by now to accept he would carry out his duty and put the word around the town that Edward, nor any of his family, were not possessed by anything. I already had a high opinion of Scabbard but it was now greatly enhance by the thought he had gone out of his way to get the strange 'doctor' to visit someone who he knew did not have the illness, just so that Edward and his family may be helped. Then I remembered what Edward had said about having special masses for young Edward. These special masses had to be paid for. The family was destitute, yet the church was making money out of their fear and desperation. *Shameful*.

Around the Town: Afternoon

Looking up at the sun I could see it was about midday now and that, for the first time since I arrived, there were clouds building in the sky. As we moved on, I noticed another building with steam, smoke and a rather unpleasant odour coming from it. I turned to Henry and asked,

"What goes on here?"

"Aah, that's where they make velum."

"Oh, really? Very interesting."

"Well, uhm, would you like to go in and have a look around?"

I thought and then, without realising the significance, said, "If Scabbard doesn't mind?"

Turning to Scabbard, I could see his confused expression and realised I had make a mistake again by treating Scabbard as an equal.

"Oh, here's Megan, sirs," said Scabbard, conveniently changing the subject, and sure enough Megan was coming up the hill carrying a large basket.

"Ah, food. Good girl, Megan," Henry called as Megan approached.

Megan smiled. "Good day, sirs. I have finished at the abbey and been back to have *another* bath and a change of clothes," she said coquettishly, tossing her head to show her lovely washed locks.

"Oh, I am pleased, Megan. Come and tell us all about it," I said.

Scabbard had already moved over to a grass verge and now took the basket from Megan and started to unpack the food and jug of small beer.

As we settled onto a blanket that had been over the top of the basket Megan had been carrying, I looked at her and she began to relate her visit to the abbey.

"I went into the abbey and immediately there was a strong smell of vinegar, so I knew things had been scrubbed and all the surfaces looked very clean. I asked about   the cleaning, about the hand washing, about staying out of the room, about the wearing and washing of masks and not touching anything unnecessarily, and the windows were all open, and they had changed the bed clothes, and there were no dead pigeons around, and there had been no blood letting, and... er... there was something else, but I have forgotten."

Megan dropped her head. "Sorry, sirs."

"No, no, that's quite all right, Megan. You have done really well," I said quickly, not wanting to dampen her enthusiasm. A smile returned to Megan's face as she lifted her head and she swelled with pride. It was probably the first time in her life that she had been trusted with an important job and she had not failed.

Then she looked at me and added, as if a casual after thought, "And then, of course, sir, I went back to the house and had another bath to make sure I don't infect anyone." She flicked her lovely newly washed hair with her fingers and gave me a flirtatious smile as I thought this was probably the first time in her life that she had ever had a bath two days on the trot.

"But, Megan, there is just one little thing you have forgotten to tell us," I said teasingly.

Megan's mouth opened and her eyes darted from side to side. Henry, Scabbard and I gazed at her for a couple of seconds in mock reproach, but then I could bear the cruelty no more and asked, "The two nuns..." I paused once more. "How are they?"

"Oh, Sister Cecelia and Sister Florence ? They are still alive and seem to be less feverish. Sister Cecelia has even been able to eat a little food."

Her audience of three heaved a sigh of relief and I wondered at Megan's casual attitude towards the improving health of the sisters. All I could think was that the assumption that I, Edmund, would make them well, had the 'white coat effect'. My father had often talked about the placebo effect a pharmacist wearing a white coat has and he often said, "Don't knock it; it works!"

At this thought, my mind was taken to my father, my mother and my sisters. What must they be thinking? They had not heard from me for days. They must be worried. When would I be able to talk to them again? Would I be back in the 21st century. before they returned from Australia? Would I ever be back in the 21st century again? I shivered at this thought and became aware that the other three were expressing their joy at this news and making Megan feel good about her part in their partial recovery. I joined in the congratulatory noises and we all sat and ate our food with a warm sense of achievement. When I had had enough to eat, I moved up the bank a little and rested my back against a tree, soaking up the midsummer rays. Once more I became aware of the fact that the picnic was not very private and that a lot of the inhabitants of Burford were watching us in a not so subtle way. Henry was obviously used to this, but I found it very discomforting.

As I topped up my suntan I noticed a group of children playing across the road and down the hill. They had a ring shaped object they were throwing against a wall. Turning to

Henry I asked, " What is the game those children are playing?"

"What, those girls down there?"

"No, those *boys,* I replied pointing to the group of children.

Boys! Exclaimed Henry sounding rather confused. They're not *boys,* they're *girls.*

"*Girls!* Surely they're all *boys?* " I questioned.

There was a long pause and eventually Henry rationalised the situation by explaining, "I think we have a translation problem here, Edmund. 'Boy' is term used to a servant, as in, "Bring me some wine, boy". Those are *girls.* They are all *knave girls.* There are no *gay girls* there. They are playing a game called coits.

"Oh!" I said hoping to terminate the conversation. I had learnt what the game was called but was now a lot more confused. It seemed *boys* were waiters, or servants, and all children were *girls.* Male children were called *knave girls* and female children were called *gay girls.* I just could not cope with this concept. For the first time the difference between 14 century language and 21st century language was just too much for me to get my head around.

When we had all finished eating, Megan began to pack up the picnic and place things back in the basket. Henry looked at her and said, "Megan, we are going to look around the velum makers. Edmund is interested in it. We will continue looking for any ailments around the town thereafter, so you may either go back to the house, and continue your duties or you may accompany us."

Megan looked at Henry, then at me and then back at Henry again.

"Ooh, er, sir, if you don't mind me coming with you… if you think I could be of any use to you, then yes, sir, I will accompany you, sir."

"That's settled then," said Henry and began to move towards the velum makers.

As we entered the velum makers, a man looked at them, saw Sir Henry and literally ran away. Thirty seconds later, he reappeared behind another man who came hurrying up to Henry saying, "Good day, Sir Henry. Good day, Sir Edmund, Scabbard." He just looked at Megan. "What brings you here, sir? How may I help you?"

"Edmund, this is Cedric, the velum master and owner."

"Good day, Cedric," I said and the man gave a little bow.

"Edmund has expressed an interest in seeing how velum is made and I told him you would be proud to show him the process."

I smiled, thinking that Henry had said no such thing.

"Oh yes, sir. Oh yes, sir. I would be very proud to do that. So, er, we shall start by looking at the hide selection process."

"Thank you, Cedric," said Sir Henry and the four of us followed Cedric into a large sort of warehouse area where there were piles of animal skins all laid one on top of the other.

The room was full of steam and there where some giant pots boiling along the side of the room. There was a very unpleasant stench that got to the back of my throat.

"This, sirs, is where we sort out those skins that are good, and those that are not good enough, go in this box here."

Henry and I looked in and muttered. Then Cedric took us over to the three giant pots, all on their own iron grates with a fire under them. A man was busy running around stoking all the fires and putting more wood under them. I got the distinct impression the man was trying to look busy.

"Here is where we boil the hides in lime to get the fur or wool off them."

Ah, lime, I thought. That explains the discomfort in my throat, but it's not the only smell. There was also the stench of the boiling hides. Above the giant pots there was a large, long hole in the wall which, presumably, served as a window and a chimney. Once more the thought of health and safety in 21st century entered my head.

Then Cedric added, "The best skins are from still born goats. They produce the smoothest parchment. Of course we need a lot of baby goats to make any small book with them."

I wondered how so many stillborn goats were found naturally or how many nannies with young were slaughtered to get at their unborn kids.

"This way now, sirs."

The party left the building through another door and into the open air. All five of us, including Cedric, took deep breaths of the fresh air to clear our lungs of the foul, acrid stench. I thought of the man inside who probably had to work there day after day, week after week, month after month, year after year. His lungs must be in a terrible state. Cedric pointed to a few washing lines that all had skins hanging on them. Apparently this was the next stage in the process.

"In here, sirs," said Cedric, opening a door to another building.

Inside was another large room with a different smell to it. As we entered there was a flurry of excitement as the unexpected visitors were noticed. Henry turned to Cedric and said, "Tell them to just carry on."

Cedric waved his hands about and the workers carried on with their jobs. All around the room were wooden frames with skins tied to the frames at many points within them. Three men were working on the skins with curved knives, scraping them. Henry looked at Cedric who took his cue. "This, sirs, is where we stretch and scrape the skins."

There was a long pause as we looked around.

"Then we tighten them again, scrape then again and stretch them again until they are the right thickness to be used."

The group spent a little time looking around and we were then led out across a courtyard with wagons and couple of tethered horses to a sort of shop.

"And this, sirs, is where we send them off to whoever wants them and some come in from the street to buy them."

We had a quick look around and soon we were back in the street giving our thanks to Cedric whose reputation in the town had probably been enhanced greatly by our visit.

"Now, where to, Scabbard?" asked Henry.

"Sir, I only know of one other family where there is definitely a sickness amongst most of the family."

"Off we go, Scabbard."

I added, "Lead on , MacDuff."

Henry and Scabbard gave me a quizzical look, but I was getting used to this. I looked towards Megan but her eyes said something different. It made me think of the adoring, well-practised gaze that the wives of American presidents give their husbands at their swearing in ceremony. We set off down the hill and into a short side street. Scabbard was leading the way and he stopped outside a little house, turning around and saying, "This is the home of Iain and Agnes and their family."

Once more the masks were passed around and tied over our mouths and noses.

Scabbard knocked on the door and it was opened by Agnes who was clearly expecting their guests and ushered us in. She looked bedraggled and not too healthy, but then again, it was always difficult to tell how old or how healthy the poor of the Middle Ages were. Inside was the usual musty, sweaty smell I had almost become use to, and there I saw Iain slumped in a chair. I approached him and asked the usual trick question used by medical people, "How are you, Iain?"

"I'm fine, thank you, sir," he croaked in a voice that clearly suggested he was in a lot of pain. Even with his hoarse voice, a clear Scottish accent could be detected.

"How long have you been in Burford, Iain?" I asked.

"Oh, many years now, sir. We came down to England during the famine to look for work."

"I see."

Then Iain added, "Burford has been good to me and my family."

I could see Henry, Scabbard and Megan were smiling with pride at the compliment from this incomer.

Everybody in the room was coughing and spluttering. Iain was feverish and smelt of sweat. The family were clearly ill but was it the pestilence?

"Please remove your top clothes, Iain."

Iain looked confused but complied with the wishes of his better. Reluctantly I lifted Iain's dirty arm and inspected his arm pit.

"Who was the first to get ill?" I asked.

"I was," said Iain. "Five days ago. I haven't been able to work since."

This was long enough to assure me the buboes would have developed by now if it were the Black Death.

"Open your mouth please, Iain, and say aah."

Iain looked confused again but opened his mouth and made the required noise. Looking into his mouth, I could clearly see spots all over his throat and tongue. "All right, Iain, you may get dressed again." I then had a quick look at all the children and Agnes but was only interested in looking down their throats.

"You have all got tonsillitis," I told them with a smile.

Silence!

"What, sir?" asked Agnes.

"Ton-sill-it-is," I said didactically. "It is a virus and not the pestilence."

Many sighs of relief and hoarse 'whoops' of joy followed.

"I expect you have had the same thing before?"

"Oh yes, sir, I have and I told people that, but no one believes me."

"Mmm, it will go away, but you need to drink honey in warm water to ease your throat. Megan will bring you some willow herbs as well and you must take the wood out of the windows and get outside as much as possible."

Turning to Agnes, I said, "All of the kerchiefs must be washed as often as possible and get some clean clothes as well."

Agnes looked embarrassed and I realised the problem was that they probably didn't have a change of clothes, so I added, "It is summer, so little clothing is needed. You can wash the children's clothes on a sunny day."

Agnes looked reassured.

"Megan can stay behind to give you advice on other things you can do."

I looked at Megan and she stood to her full height and nodded that she understood. As they were leaving, Agnes nervously asked, "Excuse me, sir, but we can't go out because other people run away from us."

"Don't worry, Agnes, Scabbard will make sure everybody knows you are all not suffering from the disease."

Scabbard looked at me and said, "I will start immediately." Then he went to the house next door and knocked on the door.

Henry and I walked off towards Burford House, our day's work completed, leaving Scabbard and Megan to carry out their allotted tasks. I looked up at the sky which was darkening by the second as the clouds moved in and began to billow. I remembered the old adage of an English summer: Three hot days and a thunderstorm. I was not particularly looking forward to the bath tub experience again, but I knew I had to set an example if I expected others to do the same. As we passed the church, we were unaware that once more we were followed by the eyes of Father MacKenzie.

20

Northleach

The next few days just flew by as we visited the sick in the town and the surrounding villages. This meant I had to get on a horse again and pretend I was a better horseman than I actually was. Anyway, it was all good practice. One of the villages to be visited was Northleach. I had been there many times before in the 21st century and was always impressed by the large church for such a small settlement. As we approached the village, there was a road block as there was at all entrances to Burford.

"*Stop there please, sirs,.*" called one of the men at the road block.

Both Henry and I reined in our horses and Henry called back, "We are Sir Henry Burford, son of Lord Burford, and this is Sir Edmund de Covny. We are both skilled medical practitioners."

The guards went into a confab and then shouted back, "Are you both healthy?"

"Yes, we are and we have come to see how the village is doing and to see if we can offer any help."

Another confab ensued and the men began to draw the barrier aside. As the two of us rode in, there was the usual forelock tugging and words of welcome.

"Is there any pestilence in the village?" asked Henry

Silence!

Then one man who appeared to be in charge said, "Well, er, we have two houses nailed up but we don't really know."

"Take me to them, now."

"To the house of sickness, sir?" he asked in surprise.

"Yes, now. Quickly, man!"

The man ran ahead, but not far into the small town to a house next to the beautiful church that looked even more dramatic in the village that had not changed much by the 21st C.. The streets were still recognisable but there were fewer of them. The man stopped by the house that had a guard outside and was literally nailed shut. By now it had become clear to me that Henry had taken control because his name carried weight that mine did not. I also realised that Henry had been very humble over the last few days, leaving me in charge in Burford.

"How are these people being fed?"

"Through here, sir," said the man, pointing to a small open window with a tray on the sill. Henry and I looked through the hole as the stench flooded out.

"Open the door!" said Henry forcefully.

"What, sir?"

"Open the door, we're going in!"

It seemed that even the birds went silent.

"*Now!*"

The men jumped and began to pull the boards off the front door as I opened the bag to get out our masks, again being watched in amazement by the men and a gathering crowd.

When we entered, we saw the family cowering and covering their eyes from the sudden light. There were two adults and four children who clearly had no idea what was going on. Henry said in a calm but forceful voice, "I am Sir

Henry Burford, son of Lord Burford and I command you to
take off your top clothes."

No one moved and after a few seconds, Henry said a
little louder, "Now!"

They began doing as they were told, still having no idea
of why they should. First I went to the father and lifted his
arm to look for buboes. I lifted up one arm first and then
the other. Having looked at him, I then moved on to the
children who were looking very afraid, but could now see
what was expected of them and that nothing bad had
happened to their father. Finally, I approached the mother
who had, naturally, been reluctant to take her clothes off.
Once more I lifted up both arms and inspected.

"You can all put your clothes on again," I said and we
both exited as fast as possible to take deep breaths of fresh
air.

The men outside backed off as we emerged and I
addressed them saying, "None of these people have the
sickness!"

Mumbling ensued and Henry took over by saying,
"None of these people have the sickness and they are no
longer to be nailed up."

A sharp intake of breath was heard and Henry added,
"They are all ill and probably infectious, so you should
avoid touching them till they are recovered, but they *will*
recover. They will stay in the house, but all the doors and
windows are to be opened."

More intakes of breath and mumbling followed.

"A servant girl will come tomorrow and she is to be
given everything she asks for and *all* instructions she gives
are to be followed," instructed Henry.

"Now take us to the other house," I commanded, trying
to don Henry's mantle of authority.

As we were being taken to the other house, I asked,
"How long have that family been in there?"

"Oh, eight days now, sir, but the other family only since two days ago, when the father returned home ill."

"Mmm. How many are in there?"

"Three children and their parents, sir."

Soon we arrived at the other house and Henry demanded the house be opened. This time the instruction was carried out immediately as Henry and I donned our masks once more. As the door was opened this time, the man in charge called in,

"This is Sir Henry Burford and Sir Edmund de Covny and you are to do as they tell you."

Inside the smell was even worse than in the last house. On the floor in a corner a man was lying motionless. I looked at the mother and kindly asked, "What is your name?"

"Daisy," she replied in a weak voice.

"Please remove your husband's top clothing."

Daisy looked very confused and frightened but began to do as she was told. The man did not respond and when his chest was revealed, Edmund told her to now help the children remove theirs and then her own.

I approached the man with great trepidation and lifted his limp arm. Immediately the stench increased and I could see the puss running down his side and arm. There was no doubt that he had the plague and he seemed to be completely lifeless. I just looked at Daisy and she began to weep saying, "He died this morning, sir."

He was clearly dead and I looked at Henry saying, "I need water before I touch the others."

Henry walked to the door and called for a bucket of water. Soon it arrived and was dropped at the door. Henry picked it up and walked over to me and I washed my hands in it before approaching the children. One child was inspected and there were no apparent buboes. Then I inspected a girl of about six years old. She was sweating and seemed to be in pain. As I lifted her arm, the small buboes became apparent. I said nothing but walked over to the bucket to wash my hands once more. Then I approached the final child. Lifting both arms, nothing was apparent and the child seemed relatively healthy. Well, as healthy as any poor child can be expected to be in the Middle Ages. Turning to Henry I said, "We must get this dead man out of here and there is no point in anyone else touching him." Henry nodded as I began to pull the dead man by his arms. Daisy and the three children burst into tears as Henry went out ahead.

Outside the crowd literally ran away as I pulled out the body. Henry washed his hands once more and then emptied the water into a nearby gully, calling for fresh water. No one touched the bucket, which was just as well, but soon another bucket of water arrived and I indicated to Henry to wash again first, ensuring no water dripped back into the bucket, before I washed in the fresh water once more. I spoke quietly to Henry. "Who is the man in charge?"

"He's the town reeve."

"The town what?"

"The reeve."

I looked confused so Henry explained, "You know, the man in charge of organising the village, planting, harvesting and anything else like these circumstances."

"Oh, I see," I said, realising this was a word everybody would have known during the Middle Ages. Telling myself that Henry would probably attribute my ignorance to my being 'foreign', I began to think that the 21st century name Reeve, or Reeves, was probably derived from this position in the Middle Ages.

"Would you tell him to arrange a quarantine house for the two children and the mother? Daisy may come back and forth to the child in here if she wants to, but if she does, she is not to have any contact with the other two children afterwards. Megan will know what to do in terms of cleaning and the washing of clothes. Tell them to also open windows and doors, but to have no contact with anyone. This must continue until either the child recovers or… dies."

Henry spoke to the reeve as I waited. Then we both mounted our horses once more. As we turned to ride away, the two children and Daisy were emerging from the house to be taken to quarantine As we did so, the sound of a very distraught six-year-old's screaming rang in our ears. This was heart-rending for both Henry and I, but it was the best we could do for the benefit of the rest of the family. Soon we were galloping along what was to become the A40 back towards Burford. At the barrier outside the town we were greeted by Scabbard who had been left behind, along with Megan, to carry out my instructions around the town.

"A bath and clothes for us both," ordered Henry and the two of us rode down the hill to go through the usual process.

Having bathed and changed yet again, Henry and I called for Scabbard and Megan to give them instructions.

"Megan, in the morning you can go and do the same things as you have done in the abbey," I told her.

"Sir, there are a few hours of light left, so I could go now and be back before midnight?"

"Well, if you don't mind," I replied, realising once more that Megan was not used to being asked if she minded being told what to do. Even so, I was once more impressed by her enthusiasm, commitment and maturity.

By the time Megan returned, both Henry and I were fast asleep.

21

Alvescot and Clanfield

At breakfast the next morning, Henry and I were joined by Lord Burford. He wanted to know what had happened in Northleach and I left most of the explaining to Henry whom I thought was coming into his own. This greater role for Henry was something that pleased me, not least because I was hoping to get back to the 21st century as soon as possible. How this was to be achieved, though, I had no idea at all. Fortunately, I had been too preoccupied with the problems of the 14th century to have given much thought as to whether or not I would ever be able to get back. After a few days I was now concerned about what my friends in the 21st century would be thinking. Most of all, my family, now in Australia, must have called my home and my mobile many times and would be upset and concerned at getting no reply. One possibility of 'escape' had crossed my mind and that was to take a horse when I was on my own and simply ride to where I had left my laptop. All I would have to do is to disappear as I had arrived and the horse was bound to return home to where his food was. That would mean my conscience was clear about the horse, but I would feel guilty about just disappearing on people who had been so good to me. Most of all, I was concerned about my good friend

Henry. Alternatively, I could tell Henry the truth and ask him to assist in my return. *No*, there was no alternative!

All these thoughts were racing through my head as Henry was relating yesterday's events to his father, and Henry's words rather faded into the background. So, when Lord Burford asked, "Do you think the young girl will survive?"

Instinctively, I just said, "What?"

There was a pause and Lord Burford asked, "Do you think the young girl with the disease will survive?"

Pulling myself back to the 14th century. I replied, "Er, that depends on many things. I am sure Megan will be able to help her a lot and I need to talk to her to see what happened last night when she went to Northleach."

"Your wish will be granted soon Edmund, as I have told both Megan and Scabbard to be here after breakfast."

As Lord Burford was finishing, there was a knock at the door and in walked Scabbard on his own. "Ah, Scabbard, is Megan not with you?"

"No sir. I have only come to tell you that Father MacKenzie is here to see you, sir." Lord Burford raised his eyebrows, saying, "I wonder what he wants. You'd better show him in."

"Yes sir." Scabbard exited.

A minute later, Scabbard showed Father MacKenzie into the room.

"Good day, Father Mackenzie, what can I do for you?"

"Good day, Lord Burford," he said with a bow. "I have some business to attend to with the bishop. Er, nothing important, you see, but I have come to beg your permission to leave the town to go to Gloucester."

"Yes, Father, of course you may, but you will be careful, of course?"

"Oh yes, sir. I may stop in Cheltenham if I can find a safe inn, but I will take great care, sir."

"Good, your trip could be useful to me as you can let me know how the pestilence goes in Gloucester on your return."

"I would be honoured to be of use to the lord," he replied obsequiously with more bowing and clenching of hands.

"In fact, I may not be here when you return as I am going to Windsor to see the king for a few days."

"Oh, I'm sure Burford will be the less without you, My Lord."

"Yes, Father, good day to you."

"Good day to you, My Lord." Father MacKenzie grovelled his way out backwards.

"Oh, Scabbard, come straight back in with Megan when you have shown the father out."

"Certainly sir."

As the door closed, Henry looked at Lord Burford and said, "I didn't know you were going to Windsor, Father."

"Yes, and that's part of the reason why I want Scabbard and Megan to be here."

Two minutes later, Scabbard and Megan entered and Lord Burford told them to sit down. Megan looked uncomfortable at this and I thought it was probably because she had never been invited to sit at the same table as the lord before.

"So, Megan, tell us about your trip to Northleach last night?"

"Well, sir, when I arrived they were obviously expecting me and they gave me all I asked for and did all I asked."

There was a long pause. "Yes, go on, Megan?"

"So, I went into the house with Matilda."

"That's the young girl?" interjected Lord Burford.

"Yes sir. And I bathed the girl, with the hot water they gave me and I covered her boils with honey. I made sure she ate something. And, er… I am afraid I, er…"

"Go on Megan."

"I, er, gave her a cuddle. Oh, I am sorry, sir, I really am sor..."

"Megan," I said, "I know I said to have as little contact as possible with the sick but Matilda is a young child and showing her love is as important as anything else."

"Oh, thank you, sir. Thank you. I did have my mask on, of course, and I washed my clothes and had *another* bath when I got back, sir."

"Good girl, Megan," reassured Lord Burford.

"Then I called for Daisy, little Matilda's mother, and told her how to go about cleaning Matilda and cleaning the house with hot water and vinegar. I also told her she could come and go between the houses but not to have any contact with her other children once she had been with Matilda. She had to choose between her children," Megan said sadly.

"It will only be for a few days, Megan, because either Matilda will get better or she... won't," I reminded her, trying to be as sensitive as possible.

"Then I went to the quarantine house and there was no comfort there, so I told the reeve to do whatever he could to make their lives better."

"Well done, Megan," praised Lord Burford. "And have you been to the abbey today?"

"Yes, I have, sir. And the sisters are progressing well. In fact, Sister Cecelia sits up in bed now."

The little gremlin got on my shoulder again and I couldn't help but ask, "Are the other sisters still praying for them?"

"Of course they are, sir."

"Well, let's move on to other matters," Lord Burford concluded.

"As some of you now know, tomorrow I am going to see the king at Windsor and I intend to tell him about what we have been doing here. I was going to take Scabbard with me but I would now also like Henry and Edmund to accompany me."

Henry sat up straight and glowed at the thought of being presented to the king. I dropped my head thinking, *How on earth am I going to handle this one?* Lord Burford went on and turned to Megan. "You, my girl, are too important here to come with us."

"Oh, thank you, sir, thank you."

"And what are you two intend on doing today?" the lord asked, turning to Henry and me.

Henry once more took command by saying, "There are a couple of important places left we need to visit – Alvescot and Clanfield – where we know people have the disease, because Clanfield was the first local village to get the disease and Alvescot is probably where the sisters got the sickness."

Lord Burford's eyes dropped at the thought of his son and heir putting himself at risk once more in a place known to have the plague. Northleach had been different, as he had not known before his son went that the sickness was definitely there.

"Well, if you are both sure it is necessary, then you must go. Tonight there will be a small celebration for the whole household."

"Oh, Father, that sounds wonderful." Then Henry looked at his father with a serious face once more and asked, "Could you spare both Megan and Scabbard today as I believe we will need their help and their horses' carrying capacity?"

"Of course they can accompany you. Scabbard, Megan, I think you both know what is expected."

"Yes, sir," they chorused.

With that they began to exit the room, but I caught Scabbard's arm. "Look, I have made a drawing and I was wondering if you could have something like this made for me?" I gave him a drawing of a basic toothbrush and pointed to the brush end. "If these could be made of the hardest bristle possible, it would be great."

Scabbard looked at it and smilingly assured me, "I'm sure this will be possible, sir."

"Good, and please make the handle as smooth as possible; I don't want any splinters."

"Of course, sir."

"Just one more thing, Scabbard... Can you get Cook to make me some sweet jelly, and then get a clean chalk stone and grind it well in a pestle and mortar and add it to the jelly in a ratio of about 1 to 3?"

Scabbard looked at me for a while and then asked, "A what of 1 to 3, sir?"

"A ratio: 1 part ground chalk to 3 parts jelly."

"Certainly, sir," replied Scabbard far too polite to show his disbelief that I wanted chalk-flavoured jelly.

Half an hour later, all four of us were on our horses and heading up the hill out of Burford. Henry was in the lead and thus dictated the route that took us across fields and not via the route that I was used to driving along. I knew we were heading south and slightly to the west of where Carterton would be established 550 years later. As we rode along, I looked to my left just to see if I could see the blue windmill I had left to mark the spot where I had hidden my laptop on that first day. It was raining a little and had been raining a lot during the night. I thought of the laptop being inside that plastic bag I had left it in, hoping that it would be enough to keep it dry. I could see nothing resembling anything blue and although I knew we were quite far away from where I had left it, I still worried whether or not a sheep had eaten it, or if a passing human had maybe picked it up thinking, 'What's this?' Anyway, there was no point in worrying now.

Soon the church was in sight, and as we approached the village, we could see there were no roadblocks to keep people out and no signs of life. The company slowed as we entered the village and stopped near the church. There was silence except for birdsong. Suddenly a voice rang out, "If you are not sick, leave as soon as possible."

We all looked around but could see no one. "Don't you know what has happened here?" the voice asked incredulously.

Henry turned towards the church where he thought the sound was coming from and replied, "Show yourself and tell me what has happened here!"

Silence.

"I am Sir Henry Burford, son of Lord Burford and we have come to see what we can do to help."

Still there was only silence. A man finally emerged from the shadows of the church. It was the priest. "God has sent his retribution for our sins. Many are dying of the sickness or are starving to death. There is a lack of food coming into the village and we cannot get out to find any. Those who are not sick or starving, are already dead!"

Henry dismounted and the others followed. "Come here and speak to me, Father Eugene. None of us has the sickness."

"Then you must leave as soon as possible, sir," was the reply as the priest slowly approached them.

"We will leave only when we have assessed the village. Now tell us what the situation is here?"

The priest clearly recognised Henry Burford and began to do as he was commanded, telling them that many households had the sickness and others remained in their houses for fear of getting the plague or being killed if they tried to go to another place. There was no point in visiting each house now, but a large barn was requisitioned and the priest went to find some men who were not ill. They came to the barn looking fearful and confused and were instructed to bring tables, beds and cooking equipment from houses where there was no sickness. Then orders were given for those in houses with the sickness, but who thought they were not ill, to come to the quarantine barn. Megan soon set to cleaning everything with vinegar and ordering fires to be set for hot water. I was struck by the difference between the nervous little girl in the presence of Lord Burford and the confident, commanding young lady in her important role. It was not surprising really. Not only was he her lord, but he literally owned her. Added to which she probably owed him her life after her parents were killed in the Welsh wars.

A few hours later, the village had been organised into sick houses and quarantine barns and houses. Henry, Megan and I all took on the task of assessing whether or not people had the sickness, as Scabbard took command of ensuring Sir Henry's other instructions were carried out. By the time they had done all that could be done, the village seemed in a much better state. Most importantly, the sense of despair and inaction had been replaced by a sense of hope. I had many times assured the villagers that not all needed to die. Eventually Henry, Scabbard and I left, leaving Megan behind to continue doing what she was now used to doing.

"You are to be back long before nightfall, Megan, as the house celebration is as much for you as anyone," commanded Henry. The final words of Sir Henry to the village were, "Scabbard will return tomorrow with more food and provisions."

This was greeted with loud cheers by the villagers who seemed transformed within the last few hours.

"But those of you who are well, must tend your fields if we are all to survive the winter."

With this the three of us turned and rode back towards Clanfield.

Within a few minutes we were approaching the small village and we could see a barrier across the road, but there were no guards to prevent our entrance. We easily rode around the barrier and stopped at what I recognised was the junction between the Alvescot and Bampton roads, but there was no Clanfield Tavern to my left. For about a minute the three of us sat in silence listening to the silence. Then Henry turned to me and said, "We think this is the first place in Oxfordshire that the plague had struck."

"Oh, I see! So, why does there appear to be no one here?"

"I can only assume it is because everybody in the village is either dead or have fled."

The full enormity of the effect of the Black Death suddenly hit me. This was what would happen to any village where the bacteria got a hold before any steps were taken to prevent its spread. No one would stay here once they knew what was happening.

There were not even any animal noises and it seemed even the birds had left.

"So, where are all the livestock?" I asked Henry.

"I imagine they were all set free before the last few people of the village left, probably in the hope they would survive and would still be around when the owners returned."

As if in answer to Henry's assessment, we heard a distant sound of a cow further down the road towards Radcot. Henry looked up towards the sound and said,

"Let's go and investigate." Then he squeezed the flanks of his horse to move on.

Slowly we moved through the few houses that constituted Clanfield in the 14th century. Soon these dwelling petered out and in a field to our left we could see a cow. She was continually mooing, but the sound was not what I was used to hearing from a cow – not that I had spent a lot of time listening to cows mooing in the 21st century! We turned off the road towards her and as we approached, she began to move away, so we reigned our horses in.

"Why is she making that strange noise?" I naively asked of Henry.

"It's probably because she has not seen men for a few days and because she needs milking. I expect she is in a lot of pain."

Of course! Henry must think I'm really thick. Everybody in an agricultural society would know that.

"Couldn't we try to catch her and milk her?" I asked with more naivety.

"Ha, ha! Well, we could try, but I doubt if she would let us catch her. She doesn't know us."

I felt I had to try something, so I passed my reigns to Henry saying, "Please hold these."

I dismounted and walked slowly towards the suffering beast. She was clearly a cow but didn't look like a Jersey or a Friesian. As I approached, she moved away so I crouched down trying to appear smaller and less threatening. I tried this many times but could never get close enough to touch her, let alone catch her and milk her. Eventually, it was clear I was wasting my time and gave up. As I returned to my horse and pulled myself back on, Henry handed me the reigns with a smile that said, 'I told you so!' Scabbard remained silent and his face said nothing. He knew his position and it was not to express an opinion on the behaviour of his betters. As we turned away, I gave one last look back to her and thought that if I had a 21st century. rifle, I would shoot her through the head to end her misery. Clearly there was nothing to be done in the village of Clanfield. In those houses there were probably dead people but there was no point in going to look. That really would be an unnecessary risk. We turned our horses and headed back towards Burford. My legs were aching a little but I was obviously getting used to riding. Before long we were approaching our destination.

As we approached the town, the usual procedure was gone through as the barriers were moved aside and every one kept their distance from the potential death we had brought with us. Then we rode down the hill, over the bridge and into the grounds of Burford House. As we dismounted, Henry told Scabbard not to rush the cleaning of the horses, saddles and bridles as he should do it properly. The other household staff could cope with the arrangements for the celebration.

"Certainly not, sir," he replied.

Once we were in the house, there were more baths and changes for all, and even I was getting a little fed up with this routine, as it was not as easy as having a quick shower in my own house, and then Henry and I met again for a brief snack before the evening's festivities. We had not eaten properly since leaving in the morning and we were very hungry. When the meal was finished I said to Henry, "I am going to my room to lie down, so I'll see you later."

"Okay," replied Henry self-consciously as I disappeared.

In my room I threw myself on my bed.

22

That Night

"*Sir*! *Sir*! It is time to get up, sir!"

I opened one eye and Scabbard slowly came into focus.

"Thank you, Scabbard."

Scabbard turned to leave, but as he was going out, I asked, "Oh, Scabbard, did you have that toothbrush made for me."

"Yes, sir, it's waiting for you with the jelly Cook has made for you."

"Good, could you bring them up along with some water please?"

I still could not prevent myself from adding 'please' to any request I made to a servant.

"Certainly sir."

I lay there for a while trying to guess the time from the fading light outside and wondering why I was so tired. I'd had plenty of sleep the night before, yet had obviously fallen asleep when all I intended was lying down for a brief moment. Was it the stress of being in this situation? The fear of catching the Black Death, or the fear of never getting back to the 21st century? Or was it the physical stress of having to do so much horse riding? It was probably a bit of everything. Then Scabbard reappeared with the toothbrush and toothpaste. He put it down on the table and walked out.

"Thank you, Scabbard." I jumped off the bed to clean my teeth properly for the first time in days.

"Sir, the barber is in and I wondered if you may like him to give you a shave?"

"Er, yes, Scabbard, that would be good."

By now I had a thin beard and although I could not grow a full beard yet, I had to admit it did look a little untidy. Obviously the lord did not *go* to the barber; the barber came to the house! He was presumably called in because of the celebration tonight. Then I remembered that I was going off to see the king tomorrow! This must be another reason why all must be shaved. There was only one bowl of water, so first I washed my hands and face as I would have to spit into the bowl when I had finished cleaning my teeth. The toothpaste wasn't too bad at all, although the bristles could have been stiffer. There was another knock at the door.

"Come in."

The door opened and a man with a large tray on which was a bowl of steaming water and various instruments entered. Around his neck were a few towels. Obviously he was the barber.

"Ah, yes, er, where would you like me to sit?"

The barber looked around at a high-backed chair and said, "Here would do nicely, sir."

I had been shaving myself for the last few years, at first rather unnecessarily, but I had never *been* shaved. First my face was washed in the hot water and then I was lathered, not very effectively, with some form of soap. A thin, very sharp knife was produced and the shaving began. It was a little painful but a not an unpleasant experience. When I thought it was all over, the process began again. Finally, my face was washed again and patted dry. Once more I found myself feeling uncomfortable. Should I pay the barber? And if so, what with? I had never had any money since being here. Fortunately, the barber packed up, gave a little bow and left.

From the noise throughout the house it was obvious things had started and I arrived just as people were sitting down to eat at the large table now laden with food. A tankard of beer was put into my hand and it soon became obvious that I was the centre of the celebration. It dawned on me that this was the first time since my birthday and passing my driving test that I was free to drink alcohol: even though I had been drinking small beer since I arrived. Now was my chance to let my hair down a little. The tankard was emptied and soon replace with another one as I became the last person to sit down at the table at the place left for me next to Henry. There were people there that I had not seen before and I was introduced, but by now the beer was beginning to have its effect and it was clearly not like the small beers I had had up to now. Then Megan walked in carrying a large tray of more food.

"Megan, you're back!" I exclaimed in a voice much louder than I should have. She smiled and began to unload her tray around the table, skilfully making her last stop next to me.

"So, did all go well in Alvescot after we left?"
"Yes, sir, I carried out all your commands and I will return tomorrow after I have been to see Matilda in Northleach."

"Good, and your hair looks lovely again, Megan."

She coyly smiled and tossed her head and then became aware that others had heard this – something I seemed completely unaware of. She smiled once more and backed out.

On the table was wine and this was the first time I had been offered wine since coming to this time. It flowed freely and I soon lost track of how much I was drinking.

Inevitably the conversation soon turned to the plague that was being visited on the world and it was incumbent upon me to express my views as to its progress. "It will sweep the whole country this year and then become less virulent during the winter as the cold kills off the bacteria."

"Bacteria," concurred Lord Burford. "Yes, you have used this word before. If I remember correctly, they are the little animals that get into people and make them ill."

"Yes, that's right. Very little, so small that they are carried inside the little fleas on the rats and they get into people when the fleas bite them. That's why we must kill as many rats as possible."

"Scabbard, how's the rat killing going?" asked the lord as Scabbard was attending to the guests.

"Oh, very well in Burford, sir, and I have set the men to do the same in Northleach and Alvescot." The conversation moved on and the wine flowed more and more.

Later the subject of the plague came up again and this time Henry asked, "Will the sickness return again after the winter?"

"Yes, it will. Even though you have had very cold winters during the last few decades..."

"Yes, I had noticed that," Lord Burford threw in.

"It will come back again. You have had colder winters, and summers, actually, because you are in what is known as the little ice age."

I was aware that the alcohol was making me say things that no one in the middle of the 14th century could know, but, because of the alcohol, I just didn't care.

"In fact, by 1350 the population of England will be only two thirds of what it was in 1347, and by the end of the century the population will be only *half* of what it was in 1350."

This information was received with a mixture of shock and disbelief, followed by embarrassed laughter.

"After that, the plague will come and go for the next three hundred years and it will not be until the 16th century that the population recovers to where it is now."

Fortunately, many had consumed even more wine than I had and this was all now being treated as drunken banter. A man down the end of the table, whose name I didn't know even though I had been introduced, asked, "So, after three hundred years, will the pestilence never return again?"

"Not after 1665, no. Well, not in England anyway."

"Why not?"

"Ah, now that *is* a good question!"

There was silence and all eyes where on me as they expected me to pontificate further. "There will be a number of reasons..."

My head was swirling and I had to try to get my thoughts together. Something told me to shut up, but I was in the flow now and enjoying it so much that nothing was going to stop me. I forced myself to go on.

"There will be better hygiene, as I have tried to teach you here, and the black rat will largely be replaced by *ratus norvegicus*..." *If only I could hear myself sounding so self-important*

"By what?" asked Henry.

"*Ratus norvegicus*, the brown rat as opposed to the black rat that is around now..."

"How will that make any difference?" added Henry.

"Well, because they carry a different sort of flea that doesn't carry the Black Death."

There was general laughter at the idea that there were different sorts of fleas, let alone that different sort of rats would have different sorts of fleas.

"And, of course, the population in general will start to develop a natural immunity to the disease."

More loud laughter. At this point, I allowed myself to drift off into my stupor and continued to stuff my face with food and wine.

Later the conversation turned to the imminent visit to see the king in Windsor. Lord Burford was the centre of this discussion and said, "I believe Edward of Woodstock..."

"Edward of Woodstock? Who's he?" I asked, jumping in rudely, as I had been told not to do, in another unguarded moment..

"Edward of Woodstock, Prince of Wales, Duke of Cornwall, Prince of Aquitaine..."

"Oh, him? The Black Prince!"

"The Black Prince? Why do you call him the Black Prince?"

Fortunately I still had just enough presence of mind to say, "Oh, er, that's what he's known as in Saxony."

"But why the *Black* Prince?"

"Er, I don't really know. It's just what he's known as."

"Ah! You have heard of his great victory over the French at Cressy, haven't you?"

"Yes, we've heard of that – some very useful Welsh archers I believe."

"Yes, they were," said Henry. "Where is Megan. Oh, there she is. Hello, Megan. She likes you, you know." Fortunately Henry was almost as drunk as I was.

Then I looked at Henry and slurred, "Do you reckon I'm well in there, then?"

"Uhm, I certainly think she likes you."

Lord Burford continued to wax lyrical about Edward of Woodstock and I chipped in, "Do you know that Cemetery Junction Station isn't really in Woodstock? It's just that Woodstock looks a lot better than Reading does."

No one took any notice of me.

"He is a wonderful prince and will make a very good king,"

"I bet you he doesn't!" I opined.

The hubbub died down and the lord spoke again. "I think you jest too much, Sir Edmund."

"I bet you a king's ransom he doesn't!"

This was close to treason and nervous laughter ran around the table.

"And his son will be a bit of an iffy character when it comes to the peasants' revolt."

"Peasants' revolt?" the man at the end of the table asked. "Why should the peasants revolt?"

"Ah well, that's all to do with the Black Death as well. You see, the plague will decimate the population so badly, as I have told you – or should that be bicimate? Hee-hee, haa-ha! – that there will not be enough peasants to work the land. So the fields will remain unsown and unharvested, and homes will remain empty, so there will be no rent imposed on them. Therefore, some lords will allow peasants, and even surfs, to work on their land and not send them back to their original manors."

More nervous laughter followed, but I just blundered on drunkenly. "Lords will even be prepared to pay *money* for their work. This will embolden the peasants and they will revolt for social, legal and political rights."

"Rights for peasants and surfs? *Haa!*" Said another man whose name I had forgotten.

Much raucous laughter followed.

"Give him some more wine, Megan," said Lord Burford.

This Megan did and I drank it with relish.

After a few courses of the meal the atmosphere changed and it seemed it was time for mutual entertainment. First, Henry's younger sister, Anne, got up and sang a little song. A nice little tune and very simple. Sounded like the sort of thing I used to listen to being sung on Children's BBC. When she had finished Lord Burford raised his hand and Megan left the room only to reappear soon with three jugs and an uncooked broad bean on a tray. He lined up the three jugs and put the bean under one of them inviting people to tell him which jug the bean was under. I had seen this trick done many times on television and by street entertainers but had no idea it was around in the Middle Ages. I suppose it's so simply it would likely be very old. I have no idea how the trick is performed so I watched in great admiration as the Lord of the Manor performed like a troubadour. Fortunately my fascination with the trick meant I kept quiet for a while.

Then it seemed it was my friend Henry's turn to entertain. As he stood, Scabbard picked up and instrument from the corner of the room and handed it to Henry. This was clearly planned and I could see it was one of the instruments Henry had shown me in the Music room. As far as I could remember it was called a viol. Henry sat down and put the instrument between his legs and began to play a tune with a bow that I did not recognise. Of course not! It seemed pretty complicated to my rather uneducated musical ear. I just couldn't get the time signature but it certainly wasn't in 4/4 time. I suddenly became aware that the room was silent. Was this out of deference for Henry's social position or was it because they were appreciative of his musical skill. When he had finished the audience showed its appreciation as did I. Once more Henry had displayed his musical abilities and I was fill with the thought that *I wish I could play like that!*

Then came the moment I was dreading – my turn to perform. What was I to do? I couldn't sing, I couldn't play any of their Medieval instruments and I couldn't do party tricks. There was just one thing I could think of; recite a poem, But which one. Once more that little Gremlin got on my shoulder and I decided to do one of Geoffrey Chaucer's so off I went.

"Experience, though noon auctoritee

Were in this world, is right ynough for me
to speke of wo that is in mariage:
For lordinges, sith I twelf yeer was of age-
Thank be God that it is eterne on live-
Housbondes at chirche dore I have had five
(If I so oft mighte han wedded be),
And alle were worthy men in hir degree
But me was told, certain, nat longe agoon is,
That sith that Crist, en wente nevere but ones
To wedding in the Cane of Galilee
That by the same ensample taughte he me
That I ne sholde wedded be but ones"

At this point I lost track of where I was and paused. This was taken to be the end of the poem and I thankfully took the opportunity to stop. Applause ensued and as I was making my way back to my seat Lord Burford asked, "Did you write that yourself, Edmund, as I don't recognise it?" Once more the Gremlin appeared on my shoulder and I replied, "No, it's written by a man called Geoffrey Chaucer and it's from 'The wife of Bath's prologue', I replied.

Oh, I've never heard of him, is he a new poet?

How should I answer this one? "Well. Sort of, but I'm sure you will hear a lot of him in a few years time"

"Mmmm, I shall try to remember his name. Geoffrey Chaucer you say?"

"Yes, sir, that's right. Geoffrey Chaucer," I hammered the point home to make sure he remembered. Chaucer was only a young boy during the Black Death so it appealed to my sense of humour, even if I had been sober, to introduce his work a few years before he had written it.

Whilst the celebration was in full swing, Father MacKenzie arrived at the bishop's palace in Gloucester and was brought before the bishop. "Your Grace, I am your humble servant."

"Welcome, Father MacKenzie. What brings you here in such difficult times?"

"There is much evil abroad, Your Grace, and I believe the Devil himself has come in the guise of a young man to Burford. His name is Edmund de Covny."

"Go on, my son."

"He speaks of causes for the pestilence other than God's retribution. He gives commands as if he were a lord or even a king."

"And what does Lord Burford say of this?"

"Well, Your Grace, he seems enthralled by the Devil's words. He gives this, this, er, heretic every assistance."

"Does he indeed?"

"In fact, Lord Burford's son, Henry, accompanies him in all he does."

"Mmm."

"He has even been into the abbey where two of the nuns are sick. They seem to be recovering, Your Grace."

"Obviously it's the work of God upon his servants."

"Yes, Your Grace, but this young man seems to wish to take the credit for the Lord Christ's work."

"Does he indeed?"

"His behaviour at mass is less than pious, Your Grace and once he seemed to suggest that we could get the disease from Holy water. He has even told a family with a child, known to be possessed by devils, that he is not possessed at all"

"Has he indeed? Mmm. His actions must be curtailed. But it will be difficult if he has the protection of Lord Burford."

"There the good Lord may have sent us a sign of encouragement."

"Go on?"

"Lord Burford is going to Windsor tomorrow to see the king and he is taking his son and the young man with him.

But he may stay in Windsor and send his son and Sir de Covny home whilst he stays in Windsor. Maybe we could, er...?"

"Yes, I see." The bishop drummed his fingers and then said, "I shall prepare a warrant for the arrest of both of them on charges of blasphemy and heresy."

"Thank you, Your Grace. I have prayed for such assistance."

"I will send some men with you and they will wait for the two young devils to return. You have done well, my son. God go with you."

At the celebration, the party was winding down and the guest were leaving. Once everyone was gone, the residents were making their way to bed but I had been slumped in a chair for a while and was snoring loudly. Henry pulled himself to his feet and looked at me. "Megan, help Edmund to bed," he said with an impish grin on his face.

"Yes, sir," responded Megan and she helped me to my feet. A few minutes later she dropped me on my bed and was walking towards the door.

"Oh, don't go, Megan," I slurred.

She walked back towards me.

"Sit down and talk to me."

She sat and I pulled myself into a sitting position.

"You do look tasty, Megan."

"Tasty, sir? What does that mean? Are you going to eat me?" She giggled.

"It means this," I said as I leant forward and kissed her.

She didn't seem to object and the little gremlin appeared on my shoulder once more. "Are you on the pill?"

"The what, sir?"

"Oh, never mind!"

23

Windsor

"Sir! Sir! Sir Edmund! It's morning, sir. Time to get up."

"Huh? What? Who? Who are you?"

"It's Scabbard, sir."

"Hooray! Can you bring me some water?"

"I have brought you some, sir. Here it is and there is honey and bread waiting for you for breakfast."

"Ooh. My tongue is sticking to the roof of my mouth."

"It will do. Come on, drink this, sir"

"Thank you."

"Everything is prepared for your journey, sir," Scabbard said and left me to my own resources. I was thankful for Scabbard once more but felt his waking me was becoming a bit of a habit.

I swilled the water around my mouth and the memory of last night slowly enter my consciousness. Then, '*wham*'! It all came flooding back. *Oh my god*! What did I say? What did I do? And Megan? What happened? Whilst this was all going through my head, I washed and dressed before making my way to the dining room. Henry was already in there, as was the bread and honey Scabbard had promised. It seemed the 14th century knew as much about hangover cures as did the 21st century.

"Hello Edmund. How are you?"

213

"Er, a little shaky. How about you?"

"About the same."

I was rather pleased to hear I was not the only one with a hangover. We chatted a little and slowly I edged the conversation around to last night.

"Did you enjoy yourself last night?" I asked Henry.

"Yes, I did. How about you?"

"I did, but I think I got a little carried away."

"Didn't we all! That's what celebrations are for." Henry opined reassuringly.

This made me feel a bit better and then Lord Burford walked in.

"Good morning, gentlemen," he said brightly. "How are you both?"

"Oh, fine!" we chanted, both trying to pretend we did not have hangovers.

"All is ready, so as soon as you are, we shall leave."

"We will be out soon," assured Henry.

Lord Burford left and we finished eating before I ran back upstairs to clean my teeth.

A few minutes later, I had my foot on the mounting block and I had to use all my strength to throw my other leg over and pull myself onto the horse. Off we went and every hoof fall made me feel as if I was being bounced up and down from a great height. We had gone out of the back of Burford House, on a route I only knew in theory, and made our way through Swinbrook and across the little bridge. I was struck by the thought that the village would change little in the next nearly 700 years. Then we went up the hill and over the Oxford road, and down again towards Bampton, which was blocked off, so we had to ride around the outskirts of the town and along the Bucklands' road. By now I was feeling like death cooled down and was sure I could not continue the ride to Windsor. When would we stop for a rest? On we went and I felt I wanted to just die on horseback. Up ahead was the river Thames and I wondered if there was a bridge there like the Tadpole bridge that still existed in the 21st century.. As we approached the river, Lord Burford and Scabbard slowed, as did my horse without any instruction. *Good*, I thought, *we are going to stop for a while.* Imagine my ecstasy when it became clear that we were going to transfer to a boat for the rest of the journey to Windsor. There was no bridge at all – just a few boats on the river.

At the riverbank there were a few men and as we approached, I thought I had seen one of them before. I soon dismissed this thought as it was silly. How could I have seen a man from the 14th century before? Suddenly I realised it was Knut, one of the two men who had picked me up the first morning. Immediately my eyes scanned the other men for Edgar who had been with Knut, and there he was. Without these two men, I would not be where I am now. I couldn't decide if that was good or bad. When the horses stopped, there was the usual forelock tugging and what felt like a special welcome for me from Knut and Edgar. I had hardly noticed the large saddle bags on my horse, and on Henry and Lord Burford's horses and the even larger ones on Scabbard's horse. Now they were being unloaded, as soon as we had dismounted, and put into two boats. The boats looked pretty large and I did not really relish the thought of rowing all the way to Windsor even if I was a member of the school rowing team. However, this did seem preferable to riding all the way to Windsor.

Once more I was delighted to find that Knut and Edgar were to accompany us as oarsmen. Lord Burford, Henry and I got into one boat whilst most of the bags were loaded into the other boat. Finally, Knut got into our boat and Edgar and Scabbard got into the other boat. Knut and Edgar picked up their respective oars. I had wondered if these boats were for hire to anyone who wanted them and this was confirmed when Lord Burford leant towards the shore and handed a purse of money to a man whom I assumed was in charge of the quay. Soon Knut and Edgar were pulling on the oars and I was pleased to lie back and rest as the two servants did the work. This was what was expected, and what they were paid for – if they were – so I decided to make the most of it and rest my hangover. The movement of the boat was very restful and the sound of lapping water on the oars added to my sense of relaxation. This was so much better than bouncing up and down on horseback.

After a couple of hours, Oxford was in sight. It was a city I knew well in the 21st century, but this was a lot smaller and all the landing stages were closed making it clear strangers were not welcome. The same went for Abingdon, but at both places Lord Burford announced himself and enquired as to the progress of the plague. It was in both Oxford and Abingdon and spreading fast. I felt compelled to try to do something, but knew I would have to start from scratch and I could not be everywhere. My next task was to have my ideas put to the king by Lord Burford and that would be far more effective overall than trying to change every town. On we went through Long Wittenham and onto Streetley, both little more than a couple of dwellings next to the river. Eventually it was beginning to get dark and all of us were very tired, Henry and I mainly because we were nursing hangovers. A riverside hostelry called the Riverside Inn came into sight where Lord Burford had rested before.

We moored the boat and Lord Burford approached the inn alone and knocked on the door. After a while a window opened and a head emerged. "Who is it"? asked the landlord.

"Lord Burford," came the simple reply.

"Oh, My Lord, I'm afraid we are closed due to the sickness."

"I understand that, my man, but you know me and none of my party have the sickness. Come and see for yourself."

"Oh, but, sir, I really shouldn't, I..."

"I will pay more than usual for the night." A long wait ensued and the lord could hear the landlord whispering to his wife.

"How much, sir?"

"Twice the usual!" More whispering could be heard.

"Very well, sir, but we will not meet you and we will put your food outside your rooms."

"That is quite acceptable to us, Landlord."

The lord then came back to the boat and explained the situation to the other five of us, adding, "I knew that with the lack of travellers recently that they would really be desperate to earn some money."

Early the next morning, we were up and out again having eaten the food left outside our doors. The day was cloudy with the odd break of sunshine that, at its low angle, made the river look like a silver road up ahead.

"We must follow the silver brick road to the land of far, far away," I said and the others just looked at me blankly. On we rowed, making good progress on the smooth water, towards Windsor. At a long, straight stretch of the water there was a track running along the riverside and I asked, "Where are we now?"

"This is a place called Pangbourne," replied Lord Burford and I remember driving along the riverbank with my dad a few times on our way to Reading to visit the Makro store. That meant that Reading wouldn't be too far ahead. An hour or so later we passed the confluence with another river and pulled in at an inn called The Jolly Fisherman. As Scabbard approached the door, it was opened and a woman said loudly, "I can provide a meal but I can't let you in."

"That's fine," replied Scabbard and soon a tray of food and beer was left on a nearby table on which some coins had been left by Lord Burford. I looked across the river and back towards the confluence and asked what the adjoining river was called. The pronunciation had changed over the near seven centuries but I managed to make out that it was the Kennet river.

"But there's virtually nothing here!" I exclaimed in another unguarded moment.

"What were you expecting?" asked Henry and the word 'Reading' passed through my mind. Fortunately it didn't come out of my mouth. Instead I just shrugged.

Soon we were back in the boat and on towards a place where we had to get out of the boat and hire some waiting locals, who kept their distance, to carry the boat around what would later become the weir at Marlow, which was a distinct, if small, settlement. Now the river was much broader than I remembered it being in the 21st century – if 'remembered' was the right verb. It stretched from chalk scarp to chalk scarp. I found this a little confusing for a while and then realised that these were the days before the Thames had been channelled. Soon we were under the cliffs at Cleavedon and I thought about Profumo and Christine Keeler but it would have meant nothing to my fellow travellers so I kept my mouth shut. The same procedure of having the boat carried was necessary at Maidenhead as well and I marvelled at the speed and efficiency with which the labourers carried the goods and the boat separately around the rocks. Payment was made into a bowl with vinegar and very soon we were back in the boat. By now the castle at Windsor had been in sight for some time and this gave Knut and Edgar an impetus to row the last few miles. By now the river was very broad and looked more like a lake. The downstream current that had helped us all the way from what I knew as the Tadpole Bridge, was now so dissipated it was virtually of no help. As we came up alongside the jetty at the heights upon which the castle was built, I looked across what seemed about a mile and could see nothing on the other side. I was thinking that those shallow, muddy waters would later become Slough. No wonder it was called 'Slough'!

There was a guard on the jetty but before the boat reached it, the cry went up,

"It is Lord Burford!"

We were welcomed and helped out of the boat with no sense of fear, unlike everyone else along the river had shown us. I wondered if our recognition was because we were expected or because the Burfords were well known at the castle. As with many things, I kept my mouth shut again but did wonder if I was being too careful. After all, a person from the far off land of Saxony would ask all sorts of questions. I looked up at the castle towering over me. It looked smaller than the time I had toured it with my parents, but it was still recognisable as Windsor Castle. We climbed up the steps but with no baggage to carry, as this was carried for us. Being inside a royal castle, rather than being on a guided tour, gave me a strange sense of unreality – but then again, my whole adventure in the 14th century had a sense of unreality to it.

On the way, Lord Burford stopped to exchange words with a few nobles we met along the way and by the time I was shown to my room, my bags were already there. It was an upper room and I looked out of the window onto the town of Windsor. The town was not very large and I could not remember what it had looked like the couple of times I had been there, but it was now partially obscured by a haze of smoke that hung over the town. The smell of burning wood was not an unpleasant one and I wondered if it was a particularly poisonous form of pollution. Then I realised that the concept would mean nothing at all to those around me now.

It was dusk by now and the setting sun was to the west side of the castle, casting long shadows across the town. I was caught up in a dream as there was a knock on the door and I instinctively answered, "Come in, Scabbard."

The door opened slowly and a stranger said, "It is not Scabbard, sir."

"Oh!" I responded, looking at the stranger and realising he must be a castle servant.

"I have come to tell you there is food prepared for when you are ready, sir."

"Oh, I will come now," I said and followed the man to a large room where a table was set out with food. Henry was already waiting. A chair was pulled out for me opposite Henry and as I sat down, Henry said, "Eat up, Edmund. We have a night of entertainment ahead of us."

I looked at Henry and thought, *Oh no, I can't stand another heavy night!* Then I looked down the table to both ends and felt incongruous sitting in the middle of a large table that could have sat twenty to thirty people. Bringing myself back to Henry's comment, I asked, "Oh yes, what's happening?"

"There is badger baiting arranged in the town for tonight."

"*What?*"

"Badger baiting."

"What? You mean in a pit with dogs?"

"Yes. All is prepared and the dogs have not been fed for days. Unfortunately, because of travel restrictions, they could not get a bear, but the fights should be good anyway."

Oh my God, I thought. *I am expected to watch dogs tearing a badger to death!* This is just too much. I have tried to fit in with medieval society but to watch that, is too much to ask.

"Oh really? Okay... Er... Would you pass the salt please?" I said, trying to change the subject. Henry passed the salt three inches across the table.

"Er, has Scabbard eaten?" I asked, trying to move things along.

"I don't know," replied Henry in a rather confused voice. "If he has, he'll be in the servants' quarters."

The meal passed with Henry doing most of the talking, telling me how his father was already with the king and telling him of what was being done in Burford and the surrounding areas to prevent the spread of the plague. Once we were full, Henry stood and said, "I will come along to your room when it's time to go."

At this point, I realised that I had been led to the dining room and had no idea of how to get back. Turning to Henry I asked him, "How do I get back to my room?"

Henry laughed and said, "Follow me. My room is not far from yours."

Off we went and it was clear Henry knew the castle well, so he had obviously been there many times.

"Here we are!" exclaimed Henry, throwing open the door to my room. "I will be back soon."

I stood in the semi-darkness. Candles had been lighted for me in my absence. I was deep in thought. Eventually I concluded that I really could not go to watch badger baiting and pretend I was excited at the sight of blood and suffering. I had seen bits of bull fights on TV and it sickened me. No only the sight of it but the thought that humans got kicks out of animal suffering. What was I to do? I paced up and down, looked out of the window many times at the lights in the town, and when there was a knock on the door, I quickly threw myself on the bed.

"Come in," I called in an affected groggy voice.

"Come on, we're all ready," called Henry

"Ooh, er. I really don't feel very well."

"What's the matter with you?" Henry asked as he entered and sat on the bed.

"My head aches and I feel so tired. I think I was asleep when you knocked."

"Well, come on, you'll feel all right once you're awake and down the town," Henry encouraged me.

"No, no. I really can't. I feel dizzy as well. I can't stand up straight."

"I know you were ill yesterday from too much wine but you seemed fine today. Come on, get up!" Henry proceeded to coerce.

"No, I really can't. I will join you later if I feel better."

"All right. If you really can't, you softie! But if you feel better, come and join us. We will go around the town hostelries later," Henry said rather despondently.

"I will certainly try," I promised lamely.

Henry stood to go, but turned and said, "You are to be presented to the king first thing tomorrow, so make sure you're better by then."

"I will," I said as Henry closed the door behind him.

I lay on my bed and thought about my new friend's love of animal suffering. I told myself that this was what was to be expected in the 14th century but even so, it upset me greatly. Although feeling ill was an excuse, it was true that I was very tired having ridden at least ten miles with a hangover and spending two days on the river over what must have been about 50 miles. I had aches in muscles I didn't know I had. As I lay there, filled with a mixture of sickness at what was happening with the badgers and sadness at the behaviour of my friend, I slowly drifted off into a deep sleep.

24

The King

Suddenly I found myself wide awake and quickly thought I may be able to join them in the hostelries. Then I realised it was getting light outside. It must be morning. I had been asleep all night. Before 5 am I guessed. What to do now? It was too early for the others to be up even though Henry had said 'first thing tomorrow'. So I lay there for a while. Soon it was fully light outside and I got out of bed and dressed. Opening the door I looked down the corridor. There was a man at the end, apparently asleep on his haunches. I walked towards him and the man regained consciousness, jumping up pretending he had been awake all the time.

"What can I do for you, sir."

"I'd like something to wash in." I was hoping to take on the mantle of authority and the right to being served.

"Certainly, sir," he replied and hurried away as I returned to my room.

A few minutes later the door was knocked and in walked the servant with a bowl of steaming water. He put it on a table and exited. I merely nodded. I washed and looked through my bag for a change of clothes that Henry had given me for my presentation to the king. Finally, I began to clean my teeth with the chalky-jelly Cook had made for me.

As I was doing this the door flew open and in rushed Henry.

"You're up early! *What are you doing?*"

"Cleaning my teeth. What's it look like?"

"Cleaning them? With what?"

I spat out the toothpaste and rinsed my mouth out before washing the toothbrush. "Toothpaste! What else?" I said, pointing to the little bowl with the paste in it. "You ought to try it. It'll help those mouth ulcers you seem to have."

"*Ulcers*! How did you know I had spots in my mouth?"

"Because you keep wincing when you eat." "Oh, all right," said Henry, taking me at my word, picking up the toothbrush and dipping it in the jelly before beginning to brush his teeth with it.

I looked on thinking about *my* toothbrush in Henry's mouth. What could I say except, "I'm sure Scabbard could have one made for you."

During breakfast the inevitable subject came up as Henry told me, "You missed a really good night last night. The badgers fought well."

"Oh did they? Never mind."

"Yes, one of them was dug out with two of her cubs. They were put into the pit with her, so she fought extra hard trying to protect them."

Although trying to avoid talking about it, I could not resist asking, "And did she succeed?"

"Well, they lived a little longer but she fought and fought until both cubs were dead and then she seemed to give up. Certainly the best fight, though!"

"What time do we see the king?" trying to change the subject.

"I think my father gave him details of your ideas and what we have done, so we shall go to court and wait to be called."

I had not given a lot of thought to meeting the king, but now the time was upon us I was filled with trepidation. How was I to behave in front of the king, Edward III?

Soon we were walking towards the great hall where the king was holding court. Inside was Lord Burford and many people were standing around waiting. At the front of the great hall was an empty throne and another empty, smaller chair next to him. Lord Burford explained to me that he had spoken to the king last night and persuaded him of the efficacy of my ideas, so there would be little for me to tell the king but that the king wanted to meet the man with the strange ideas.

We stood around waiting for literally hours which annoyed me, but didn't seem to annoy either of the Burfords. They probably just accepted their lowly position of waiting for the king. Eventually, the herald announced, "His Majesty the king, and the Prince of Wales!"

Silence fell, and the king, and the Prince of Wales – later to be known as the Black Prince – walked in. This was the man I had, foolishly, bet would not make a good king. I wondered if anyone would ever remember my words when Prince Edward was to die just before his father died. Much business was conducted by the king as everyone else waited. This made me even more bored, but what could I do? Then the herald announced, "Sir Edmund de Covny."

I froze and Lord Burford gave me a gentle push forward. I approached the throne and did as I had seen others do. I bowed my head and said, "Your Majesty."

"Ah, de Covny!" I raised my eyes apprehensively. "Burford has told me about you. You are the young man from Saxony, aren't you?"

"Yes, Your Majesty."

"I have been there!" *Oh no*, I thought. He probably knows more about the place than I do!

"Good hunting!"

"I'm glad you think so, Your Majesty." Then I wondered if this sounded too cocky.

"Well, I have listened to what Burford had to say and your ideas certainly seem to have merit to them."

I smiled and kept my mouth shut.

"I have ordered the vinegar cleaning regime, set up the quarantine area of the castle, ordered the killing of the rats and sent out orders to surrounding towns and villages to bring back any cats and dogs."

"This is a good start, Your Majesty." Once more, I was wondering if this was too presumptuous.

"We shall see how the plague progresses in the town?" the king enquired, presumably rhetorically.

"Your Majesty, it is important that such things are done *everywhere* to avoid the spread of the disease."

The king looked at me and I realised this probably was stepping outside my 'position'.

"All that is necessary shall be done," responded His Majesty with a finality in his voice.

I lowered my eyes. "Your Majesty."

The king made a slight movement with his hand and I realised I was dismissed. I backed out following what I had seen others doing, and when I reached the surrounding audience, I turned and walked, heaving an audible sound of relief as I heard the herald announce, "Lord Burford and Sir Henry Burford"

This came as a surprise to me and Lord Burford passed me with a smile which made me feel better as he approached the king. Henry didn't catch my eye.

"Ah, my Lord Burford!"

"Your Majesty," came the obligatory response with a low bow.

"So, you will be staying here for other matters of state but your son and, er, er, the other one, may return to Burford."

"Majesty."

Another slight movement of the hand from the king and Lord Burford, along with Henry, backed away, as I had done, so I assumed I had got it right. As they reached the audience the two Burfords joined me. Then we all proceeded to the back of the great hall and exited.

"Well done, Edmund!" exclaimed Lord Burford and I realised that despite my nervousness, I had passed the test.

"Go and eat before you go out to the town tonight, but do not get carried away. You must be up early again tomorrow to return to Burford. I am staying here for a few more days and Scabbard and Edgar are staying with me, but Knut will go with you."

Once more a sumptuous meal was presented, fit for a king – literally. When it was finished it was late afternoon and I wondered what I had done with the day. The obvious answer was that I waited to be spoken to for a couple of minutes by some bloke with a metal Christmas hat on who was holding a ball while some other bloke supported his hand. What a way to live! Henry and I returned to our respective rooms and I waited until Henry came to get me. Whilst I was pleased to have avoided the blood bath last night, I was sorry to have missed out on the pub crawl, so I was looking forward to going out this evening.

Early that evening Henry came for me and as we approached the castle gates, we met two other young men whom Henry clearly knew. Henry introduced them to me: Sir John Fitzroy and Sir Richard Grosvenor. Immediately I wondered if this was an ancestor of the 21st century. Grosvenor, who was the richest man in Britain, and thought about how the chance of someone being one of William the Conqueror's hangers on could end up being the inheritor of the world's most valuable piece of real estate nearly a millennium later. The town was not very big and there seemed to be only three inns worth visiting, which was just as well, as we had to be up early the next morning. The craic was good but I felt uncomfortable when each time we entered an inn and all fell silence as if we were intruding on something. Obviously the locals felt intimidated by the presence of their 'betters'. The town was far from empty but Henry observed, "Windsor is usually a lot more lively, but people are afraid to go out more than is necessary for obvious reasons."

I added to this observation, "It probably doesn't help that we are from outside the town and may be infected."

"No, it doesn't," added Grosvenor, and he and Fitzroy fell into drunken giggles.

I realised they had already consumed a lot of beer before we met up and looked at Henry. Catching his eye, I motioned towards the door.

"Oh, just one more, Edmund."

"All right, but don't forget we need to be up at dawn."

"Yes, but it is still early evening."

I just stared at him. "Oh well, just one more. I don't want another bollocking from your dad."

"A what?" asked Henry and I ignored him.

Fortunately he was too pissed to pursue the matter.

"More beer, Innkeeper," called Grosvenor and more was produced.

We chatted but I have to say it was a little boring being sober with two well oils people and although Henry was not that far gone he managed to get into the swing of things – behaving drunk even if he wasn't. I felt the same way as I did when I was the driver in the 21st century; not really part of what was going on and I certainly did not want to feel the same way I had travelling down from Burford. I had learnt hangovers are not pleasant things! I drained my tankard and looked at Henry again. "Sorry to be a party pooper."

"A what?" enquired Henry.

Amidst more drunken giggles, Fitzroy added, "I was also wondering about that."

"Oh, all right. Okay! We shall leave now," said Henry, producing some coins he placed on the table as the two of us left, bidding goodnight to Grosvenor and Fitzroy.

Back at the castle Henry and I went to our separate rooms. I lay in my bed for a while thinking of having been 'presented' to the most powerful man in medieval England. Soon I was asleep.

As the sun began to rise, Scabbard was standing over me with a bowl of hot water in his hands.

"Good day, sir. It is time to rise."

"Mmm. Er. What? Oh yes, thanks Scabbard."

"Your water is here, sir. Do you need anything else?"

"Umm, no. I didn't have much to drink last night."

"As you wish, sir. There is food waiting for you and Sir Henry," he said and left the room.

I washed and dressed quickly, glad that I had got to bed early before another couple of days on the river. Outside my room the same servant was waiting as the morning before and he showed me through the maze that was the castle to the breakfast room. To my surprise, Henry was not there and I asked the servant, "Where is Sir Henry?"

"I do not know, sir, but I believe he is just not ready yet."

"All right," I replied and sat down to eat.

It was not long before Henry turned up and we both chatted a little about the day ahead as more and more food was brought in for us, presumable to prepare us for the long row ahead, even if we were not doing the rowing. After we had eaten, I said,

"I'll just pop back and clean my teeth before we go."

"I'll do mine too. I enjoyed that yesterday." I wished I hadn't mentioned it!

How long would it be before Scabbard could have one made for Henry?

Outside my room the servant was waiting once more to carry my bags but I made sure I took time to wash my toothbrush again before I cleaned my teeth. Not that that made any difference because I would still have to use it again after Henry had cleaned his teeth. It just seemed a little better. Henry watched me brushing my teeth and asked, "Don't you have to do it for a long time?"

The gremlin appeared on my shoulder once more. "Five minutes if it's not an electric one."

Henry didn't ask. When I had finished he picked up my toothbrush without asking and proceeded to clean his teeth. I tried not to notice but my tummy turned. I'm sure it's 99.9% a psychological thing as it will be washed before I use it again.

Having finished Henry opened the door and motioned to the servant who picked up the bags and walked down the corridor. We followed the servant down and Scabbard was waiting for us at the back gate with another man. Scabbard explained, "Sirs, this is Matthew. He, along with Knut, will be accompanying you to help with the rowing to where you change to horses. He will be in a slightly smaller boat as you have less luggage than when Lord Burford was with you on your journey to Windsor. Then he will bring the boat back."

"Good day, Matthew," I said acknowledging the man.

Henry seemed to know Matthew.

At the quayside Knut was waiting and I said, "Good day, Knut."

"Good day, sir," he replied.

As Henry and I started down the step to the boats, followed by Scabbard, Knut and Matthew carrying the luggage, we heard, "Henry! Henry! Wait, Henry!"

It was Lord Burford.

"I just wanted to say farewell," he panted as he approached the quay.

"Oh, thank you, Father, and farewell to you," Henry replied, going back up a couple of steps.

"The journey back will take you longer because you are going upstream, so I suggest you stay the first night where we stopped yesterday near the river confluence and the second night, well, I have stayed at an inn at Wittingham a few times. The landlord will know me."

"All right, Father. Fare you well."

"Fare you well, Henry. Fare you well, Edmund."

"Fare you well, sir," I responded.

It seemed as if Matthew didn't exist.

25

The Bishop's Men

We boarded the boat and pushed off, waving to Lord Burford. It had not occurred to me that the return trip would take longer because it was upstream. The only rowing I had done before was on the Cherwell river in a hired boat or with the school's rowing team on a lake. I didn't have to row now, as that was what Matthew and Knut were for, but I liked the idea and told everyone saying, "When it's convenient, I would like to do a bit of rowing."

Silence fell except for Henry who gave a little giggle.

I looked at him and said, "I enjoy rowing! I do it in the school team and I'd like a bit of practice."

Knut and Matthew said nothing. What could they say? Eventually Henry said,

"Well, if you want to."

It was settled.

Even against the flow we seemed to make good time and soon we were at the rocks near Maidenhead. The same men were there to carry the boat and soon we were on our way once again. The same procedure followed at Marlow and we ate whilst the boats were being transported past the rocks. By early evening, we were at the Fisherman's Inn once more. Henry and Edmund approach the inn and a window was opened. "You want the same as yesterday, sir?"

"Yes, but we'd also like to stay the night."

"Ooh, well, sir. I don't know about that? I, er..."

"We will have no contact with anyone and will pay twice the normal amount."

"Well, sirs, I think we could allow that."

The food was eaten and the beds were found as night fell.

The next day, we were up, breakfasted early and got into the boat as quickly as possible. It was an overcast day and there were a few spots of rain in the air. Matthew and Knut shared the rowing but I did insist on rowing sometimes. Henry, to my surprise, also joined in on the other oars. I think he just wanted to accompany me. Knut and Matthew seemed to be uncomfortable. Why keep a dog and bark yourself? They must have been worried they were becoming redundant. We were through Pangbourne and by now the spots of rain had turned into continuous rain. There was nothing we could do and we ate as we rowed to save time so that we could get to the Riverside Inn again where we could rest. We rounded a bend early afternoon and there it was. By now it was raining quite hard and Henry and I ran towards the inn leaving Matthew and Knut to moor the boat. Once more a window opened and a voice called out, "You want to stay the night again, sirs?"

"No, just something to eat and a fire to dry ourselves by," replied Henry.

"Oh, sirs, we have no fire lighted it being summer and all."

"Then light one man! You know we will pay well!" came the rather short reply as Henry was getting tired of the negotiation theatrics.

The sound of bolts moving followed soon and the door opened as the innkeeper stepped back saying, "Wait here whilst I light a fire, sirs."

The two of us began to remove our outer clothing as the door open again and Matthew entered with some of the bags. "Good man," said Henry.

"Scabbard is bringing some more and I will get the rest of the bags, sir," replied Matthew and disappeared again as Knut pushed past him.

As he returned, the innkeeper came back as well saying, "Follow me please, sirs."

He took us a few steps down the corridor and pointed to an open door with the glow of a fire emanating from it.

"Thank you," said Henry a little less irritably this time.

"I will bring you food, sirs." Then he closed the door.

We placed our wet clothes on the backs of chairs around the fire and tried to dry ourselves. There was a knock on the door and instinctively I said, "Come in!"

There was no reply and Matthew opened the door to find two trays of food waiting. We ate slowly, as we were in no rush to go back out into the rain, and as we did, the rain seemed to be easing off. A couple of hours after we arrived, Henry put some coins on the table, and we were making our way towards the boats again. By now the rain was merely a light drizzle as we pushed off from the jetty. A voice rang out from the inn, "Thank you, sirs! You are welcome again."

On we rowed again, through Streetley and towards Wittenham. I now remembered that I had been there once before when I was about 12 years old. My father had taken me and a friend to one of the music sessions he went to in a pub, but instead of a stage with microphones and amplifiers, there were just a load of old men sitting around strumming guitars. I couldn't remember the pub's name and it certainly didn't look nearly 700 years old. As night began to fall, we approached Wittenham. Lord Burford had been right, it would take us three days to get back and we were only just making Wittenham before nightfall. It must be nearly 10 pm Again Henry and I walked up to the inn leaving Matthew and Knut to tie up and unload the boats. It was a few hundred yards to the inn and Henry knocked on the door.

"Good day," I called as by now I had learnt that 'hello' just got me strange looks.

There was no response, so Henry called out, "I am Sir Henry Burford, son of Lord Burford. My father said you would give us shelter for the night."

We waited and then a door opened. A man stood there saying, "I am sorry, sir, but we need to be careful these days."

"I understand," replied Henry.

This man seemed less frightened than the last landlord had been. Perhaps it was because he knew Lord Burford, and it made us all feel more human and less like lepers. The food was good and the beds were soft. Early the next morning, I went out to the front of the inn before breakfast to look at the village. There were just a few little houses and a couple of larger ones. I had distinctly remembered the sharp speed bumps as we had driven through the village in the 21st century but, of course, there were none there in the 14th century. When I was back in the inn I said nothing to Henry about my little nostalgia trip as we ate breakfast. There was no need to make life more difficult than it already was.

After breakfast we got back in the boats for the final leg of the journey and we made good progress through the morning towards Abingdon. Again it was not a sunny day, but at least it was not raining. We rowed through Abingdon and around the small city of Oxford. People watched us from the river bank as we passed but we took little notice and no one in the boats spoke to the watchers. As Oxford faded in the background, I thought it wouldn't be long now until we were back at the Tadpole bridge. But the last few miles seemed much further than I had expected and soon after we had passed Oxford, Henry spoke to suggest, "One last stop to eat before we get to the horses?"

Matthew caught an overhanging branch and tied the boats up before he opened the last of the food and drink. Henry and I both got out of the boat but only really to stretch our legs. From the brief appearance the sun made from behind the clouds, it looked as if it was early afternoon and I was overcome with a desire to be home and have a watch to look at. Apart from the worry of my parents, I was simply home sick. When, and how, would I ever get back to the 21st century? Having filled our tummies and stretched our legs we were back in the boats and Matthew and Knut were rowing hard. On we went but the two rowers began to slow their pace.

"We will take over for the last stretch, Matthew," offered Henry.

Matthew embarrassedly said, "Thank you, sir." He looked very uncomfortable once more.

Why had Henry done this? Was he just taking his cue from me or was he as eager as I to get back?

Both of us were rowing now and, although we were both fresh, we were not much faster than with Knut and Matthew rowing, having been going for many hours. Half an hour later we rounded a bend and the tethered horses came into sight. My heart jumped and I put a final spurt into my effort. We slid onto the river bank as one of the men caught the rope thrown by Matthew. The two of us sat on a couple of stones on the bank, as the grass was wet, and rested as Matthew and Knut transferred the bags to the same horses we had come down with a few days ago.

"Will Matthew have to take the boat straight back today?"

"No, he will stay the night in Chimney and go back tomorrow. It will be a lot quicker without us and the baggage in the boat and, of course, it is downstream."

Before long, the horses were packed and Henry paid the men. As he returned to me and the horses he said, "There have not been many travellers recently so I gave the men a little extra. Why should the innkeepers be the only ones to get extra."

This showed Henry's kindness but I could not help but think of the badgers and the cubs being torn to pieces for his entertainment.

"Farewell, Matthew," called Henry.

"Farewell, Matthew," I called. "And thank you."

"Oh, thank you, sir."

Henry kicked his horse into life and my horse followed without encouragement.

I remembered how painful the journey out had been when I had a hangover. The journey back was much easier but, even so, my muscles were complaining about the work they had had to do over the last few days. We rode through Chimney and the small village, just a few houses, appeared to be deserted. Beamtoon, as Henry called it, appeared up ahead and, as before, we had to go around the town. As we came into Brize Norton I desperately wanted to turn left and go home, but knew I could not. I was thinking of home more and more. Was this just because I was so tired? How would I feel tomorrow? Without giving it any thought I slowed my horse and Henry became aware I was lagging behind so stopped to wait for me. "Why are you stopping he asked?"

"I just think St. Britius is a beautiful church," I explained in a half truth.

"St. who?"

"St. Britius" I responded stating the obvious.

"Who is St. Britius?"

"The saint to whom this church is dedicated!"

"This isn't St. *Britius.* This is St. Peter's church," Henry said matter of factly.

"Oh! My mistake." I said embarrassedly. Obviously the church name has changed since the middle ages. Henry didn't seem to take much notice of my error and once more I reminded myself that only I knew the truth of my origins. Henry would just think it was simply an understandable error of a foreigner.

"Let's get on," urged Henry.

"Yes, no time for sightseeing!"

"*Sightseeing?*" Questioned Henry. Realising that I had made yet another time warp mistake I thought, *The middle ages had no concept of sightseeing. The closest they would come to the idea would be to go on a pilgrimage and marvel at churches because they were works of God not simply for their architecture.*

I ignored his question and squeezed my knees to urge my horse on.

Then we rode up the hill and I looked back to where Carterton should be. My heart ached but Henry was up ahead and I had to follow him. We went over the Oxford/Gloucester road on the crest of the hill and down the other side into Swinbrook. A man was walking by the roadside and stood aside to allow us to pass. As we did, the man waved, probably recognising Sir Henry. With a sense of great joy we turned into the back of Burford House. Henry was pleased to be back home and I was pleased to be back - even if it wasn't home. We dismounted and I looked at Henry who was clearly less exhausted than me. Living in the Middle Ages was perhaps fitter and healthier in some ways.

Knut didn't look at all tired and he immediately began to unload the horses.

Lady Burford emerged from the house saying, "Henry! Henry, you are back!"

"Yes, Mother, we are."

"Oh, I am so pleased to see you." Then she added as an afterthought, "And you, Edmund!"

One by one Henry's siblings, Anne, Marion and John appeared to greet their brother and his friend. We entered the house and Lady Burford disappeared to organise a meal for the returnees. As Henry and I went upstairs together, leaving the three younger Burfords behind, Megan appeared at the top. "Sirs! Sirs, you must get out immediately!"

"Oh, Megan, good to see yo..."

"Sirs! Sirs, you must get out immediately!"

"What are you talking about!" exclaimed Henry, and I just looked confused at Megan's distressed state.

"The bishop's men are in the church and waiting for your return without the lord so that they can arrest you both for blasphemy and heresy," she gabbled.

"*What*? That's ridiculous," I said.

"No, no, no, sir. It is true. I am friends with one of the altar boys and he told me."

"Aah, that's silly," I added.

Then I looked at Henry who had turned white. There was a brief silence and then Megan started again.

"Someone in the town will have seen your return and word will soon reach the church. The father has made a complaint about you both to the bishop and they are waiting for you. My friend overheard them talking and told me at great risk to himself. If Father MacKenzie finds out he will..."

I looked at Henry again who was still white and apparently dumbstruck. Eventually he said, "She is right. We must get out and hide until my father returns."

My jaw dropped and Henry turned to Megan.

"You haven't told my mother, have you?"

"No, sir, I haven't told anyone. I didn't dare."

We all stood there in silence for a few moments as we thought. Then I said to Henry, "Well, I know where I can go, but I can't take you with me, Henry."

"Why can't you?"

"I can't."

"Why?"

"I can't explain why, but I can't."

"Where?"

"It's not far away, but I can't take you, Henry," I said more forcefully.

"Why not?"

"Because..."

Just then, we heard a loud knock at the door.

"That'll be the bishops' men! That'll be the bishop's men," Megan screamed in a hushed voice. "You must go!"

"You must take me with you, Edmund."

"I can't."

"Go now. Go now!" pressed Megan.

Henry looked at me.

"All right, come with me but I don't know what will happen."

"Good man, Edmund."

The door was banged again, louder, and we could hear footsteps going towards the door.

"I will try to hold them whilst you get out the back," said Megan as she turned to run down the stairs.

"Megan," I called and she turned around.

I bounded downstairs, grabbed her and kissed her full on the mouth before she turned and ran down the last few stairs.

Henry and I ran through the house, down the back stairs and out into the yard again. The horses were still standing there steaming with a man just about to take them into their stables to be brushed down.

"Leave them," shouted Henry and the man reeled around in surprise.

We jumped straight onto the mounting blocks and the horses where kicked off into an immediate gallop. Henry was in front but I drew alongside and shouted, "Let me lead the way; I know where to go."

Henry slowed slightly and I shot ahead. Into Swinbrook we sped and over the bridge. Then we were up the hill as fast as the horses could gallop and I, being extremely tired, hung on for dear life as the adrenalin of fear gave me that extra bit of energy I needed. We reached the top and crossed over Oxford road into the direction of where Carterton would start to grow in 550 years' time.

"Where are we going?" shouted Henry, but I gave no reply.

Now I could see the rough track to our right and turned to follow it.

"Where are we going?" shouted Henry again, but I had no time to explain.

Now I could see the crossroads ahead and as we went over it, I turned my horse slightly to the right heading south east. Then I slowed and started looking around for the blue windmill.

"Where are we going?" Henry asked again, but I just kept riding slowly back and forth.

"What are you looking for?" asked Henry.

Still, I gave him no response.

"What are you looking for?" Henry asked again, more exasperated this time.

"A blue windmill," I replied.

"*A blue windmill*! Why would a windmill be blue?"

There was no response from my side.

"The bishop's men will soon follow our hoof marks and will catch us."

I continued to ride back and forth.

"Why are you wasting time, Edmund? *Please, Edmund!*"

I was engrossed in my search.

"We must go on, Ed..."

"*There it is!*" I 'whooped' and trotted a few yards. Then I dismounted.

Soon I found the hedge under which I had hidden the laptop in the plastic bag and pulled it out. As I was opening the plastic bag and taking the laptop out of its case, Henry screamed, "*There they are!*"

I pressed the power button and the screen came to life.

"*What are you doing, Edmund?* We must go *now!*"

The screen started to load the icons and now we could hear the hooves of the approaching bishop's men's horses. I had not turned it off so it was only in hibernation state so was quite quick to come back to life. Even so, it seemed like hours

"*Come on, Edmund! What are you doing?*"

I just sat there crossed-legged with the laptop on my thighs.

"You'll get us both killed, Edmund!"

"Get off your horse and come here, Henry."

"*Don't be silly, Edmund. It's the stake for us it they get us!*"

"Don't argue, Henry, just do as I say. It's our only chance."

We could hear the horses' hooves slow as the men came closer.

"Now, Henry, or I'll have to go without you."

"Go where?" asked Henry as he found himself dismounting but not really knowing why.

The horses' hooves stopped as Henry reached my side.

"Sit in front of me and hold onto the other side of this."

Henry said nothing, as it was too late to ride away, and put his fingers and thumbs around the bottom of the laptop lid. I moved the pointer to the 'undo' button as the bishop's men dismounted, swords drawn.

"Hold on tight," I commanded, "and don't let go no matter what happens. This may take me, it may take us both or it may take neither of us," I said as I pressed the 'enter' key.

The letters in the address bar moved and mist swirled around us both as the bishop's men saw us disappear into thin air.

THE END